UNDERCOVER LOVE

LUCY SCORE

That's What She Said Publishing,Inc.

ISBN: 978-1-945631-18-4 (ebook)

ISBN: 978-1-945631-19-1 (paperback)

lucyscore.com

030120

11

_a_shley grimly gripped the handle of her coffee mug as she stared out at the gray scene beyond the loft window. Rain pattered on the glass and thunder rumbled in the distance.

The dreary sky matched her mood.

Mind spinning, she had driven herself home and tossed and turned for the better part of the night. Someone—most likely Jason—had poured Steven into a cab that brought him home. She was thankful that he had made it only as far as the couch before passing out cold.

When she stood over him early that morning, she had to restrain herself from choking him awake. She settled for shoving him onto the floor.

And when he mumbled "'Toria" in his sleep, she stormed back into their bedroom and took a seam ripper to the pockets of every pair of pants that Steven owned.

The meticulous task helped temper her furious desire for blood down to a strong craving for revenge. He was in the shower now, blissfully unaware of the internal battle Ashley was fighting.

Spy or kill?

"Morning, babe."

She tensed as he came up behind her and brushed a kiss across her cheek. "Oh my God, that coffee smells amazing." He made his way into the kitchen, and she turned to watch him pour himself a mug. "So last night was pretty crazy, right?"

Her glare bored holes in him, but Steven was oblivious. "Pretty crazy," she agreed mildly.

"Sorry you had to drive yourself home."

"It wasn't a big deal," she said, sipping her coffee. Ashley watched him grab the sugar bowl and heap several spoonfuls into the travel mug. "Are you going somewhere?"

"Yeah, I've got a work thing for lunch."

Get him to talk about work. Jason's words echoed in her head. "Wow. On a Saturday? You've been really busy at work lately. Is it paying off?" The words stuck in her throat like too much peanut butter, but she forced them out.

Steven paused briefly without making eye contact. "I'm actually thinking about looking at other opportunities," he said, screwing the lid onto the mug.

"Any opportunity in particular?" She tried to keep her tone light.

"You're not pissed?" He looked suspicious.

"You've invested a lot of time at work and aren't getting ahead fast enough." It was as fake nice as she could get, given the circumstances, but the sniveling, stupid weasel bought it.

"That's exactly it! I've been there four years, and they just keep telling me to 'be patient' and 'work hard.'" He waved dismissively. "If they don't think I'm partner material, there are plenty of other places that will."

She bit her tongue and nodded. She was pretty certain he was parroting Victoria.

"Anyway, I've gotta get going. You working today?"

"Yeah."

"I'll see you later then. Text me and let me know what the plan is for dinner."

He grabbed his keys and wallet and waved over his shoulder on his way out the door.

Ashley let out a breath, only partially relieved that she hadn't given in to her murderous tendencies. She went back to pensively drinking her coffee. Her phone signaled from the kitchen island.

Jason: Do you need me to come over with a shovel and a body-sized rug?

The text almost made her crack a smile. Almost.

Ashley: Not yet. He's still alive. Barely. Says he's looking at other employment "opportunities."

Jason: Interesting.

And then a few seconds later...

Jason: How are you?

She ignored the text. She already knew she couldn't trust Jason. The man's Plan A had been to make out with her and then blackmail her into helping him. But their interests were currently aligned. It was just simple a business relationship.

Two hours later, Ashley pushed open the shop door and

paused to let the familiar scents, the charming order, envelop her. A corner unit, the store had windows on two sides and complemented the flood of natural light with chic industrial ceiling lights. It was a bright and airy space with light hardwood floors and whites, linens, and ecrus acting as a crisp backdrop to the treasures and pieces owner Barbara Estep found in her travels.

Ashley always found it to be a soothing atmosphere, even with the constant bustle of customers. This was home. And she was determined not to let anything else in her life ruin this place for her.

"Hey, boss lady!" The cheerful greeting came from the willowy redhead behind the register. At fifty-two, Janice didn't look a day over thirty-five. She dressed like an artist and moved like a dancer. Her wardrobe flowed, and her accessories made their own kind of music.

Today, she was dressed in cropped pants with a gauzy tunic the color of limes. Her fire-engine curls were pulled back with a jade green scarf, and she wore a half dozen hammered copper bracelets on her wrists.

"Hi, minion. How's it going so far today?"

"A little slow customer-wise. But we had two ladies come in and drop a pretty penny on the hand-carved armoire and two sets of the organic cotton bath linens. One of them definitely had her eye on the vase in the front window. She'll be back for it," Janice predicted.

Ashley smiled. She came to Dwell two years ago, fresh out of college and ready to tackle the retail world. Barbara, the store's owner, hired her as assistant manager and immediately began grooming Ashley to take over one day. Six months ago, Barbara had named Ashley manager and increased her own traveling time.

This month, Barbara was in Morocco, and her last email

included a few pictures of pieces that Ashley couldn't wait to slobber over before putting them out on the floor.

"Do you need anything before I head back?" Ashley asked, gathering up a few files from behind the register.

"Nope, I'm good. I'll call you if anything interesting happens. Have fun in The Cell!"

"The Cell" was the staff's affectionate name for the tiny, but obsessively organized back office. It was a windowless room barely bigger than a walk-in closet. Two sets of industrial shelving with office supplies and equipment occupied one wall. The writing desk, feminine in its subtle curves, stood in the center of the room.

Two Saturdays a month, Ashley closeted herself away in The Cell to focus on paperwork and planning. She sank into the cool leather of the desk chair and paused for a moment to rest her head on the desk.

"My personal life will not affect my professional life," she repeated quietly. A few deep breaths later, and she almost believed the mantra.

She took half an hour to schedule out a week's worth of Facebook posts and tweets for the store, announcing Tuesday's sale on glassware and posting a few of the pictures from Barbara's trip. She scrolled through Instagram, answering a few questions in the comments. Fun done, Ashley reviewed and submitted the payroll online and then moved on to email the inventory report to the accountant.

Making her way down the list, she approved a magazine ad, responded to several customer questions, and was working her way through the special requests and orders when she paused to check her phone.

Six texts.

One from Dead Guy Walking.

Steven: Dinner with the guys at Woody's tonight. Want to come?

And the rest from Jason ending with:

Jason: You can't avoid me forever.

She rubbed her hands over her face and tried to ignore the dull throbbing behind her eyes.

She needed a night out. A few hours away from the disaster that had become her life. And she knew exactly who to call.

"Do my eyes deceive me or does your Facebook status say you're home?"

"ASAP! Please tell me I can see you tonight!" Her best friend's greeting exploded through the phone, making Ashley grin.

"I'm up for a night out if you are."

Georgie's laugh eased some of the tension around Ashley's heart. Friends since high school, they had stayed in touch through college and ensuing careers and moves. Georgie was something of a club promoter who traveled constantly checking up on businesses owned by her company and scouting out other establishments for acquiring or competitive assessments. As Georgie liked to say, she was paid to party four nights a week.

"Well, it just so happens I have some research to do at Launch tonight. Are you in?"

"God, yes."

"Sounds like we have a lot to catch up on. Is everything okay?" Georgie demanded.

Ashley sighed. "I'll explain everything tonight over tequila. Lots and lots of tequila."

"Then you'd better come to the hotel early, and we'll play dress up while you spill your guts."

She felt gratitude well up in her chest and fight against the black cloud that had taken up residence there. "I can't wait to see you. I'm really glad you're here."

"Me, too, Ash."

When Ashley hung up, she realized Georgie hadn't asked about Steven. It wasn't really a surprise. She had never been much of a fan of him since he made a pass at her during a weekend visit with Ashley when they were sophomores. He'd made a compelling "I was wasted" argument, apologized profusely, and Ashley had forgiven him.

But Georgie hadn't forgiven or forgotten.

12

_a_t seven on the nose, Ashley stepped into the marble-floored hotel lobby through the heavy revolving door. The two-story space was accented by huge potted plants surrounding a dramatic fountain that burbled and spat in the way only classy water features did.

"Ashley!"

She turned in the direction of her name and was nearly mowed over by a blur of honey blonde hair and long, tan limbs.

"Georgie! I am so glad to see you! You have no idea."

Georgie threw her arms around Ashley and squeezed.

"I am so glad you called! I'm only in town for the weekend, and I wasn't sure if you'd have time for me!" She pulled back and squished Ashley's face between her hands. "You. Look. Great."

"I look great? You look amazing!" It came out mumbly through her compressed cheeks.

Georgie shrugged off the compliment. "That's what a week in Ibiza does for you. Now, come upstairs so we can catch up!"

She half dragged Ashley to the bank of elevators, waving a friendly hello at the front desk staff.

"This place is gorgeous," Ashley said, leaning against the elevator's railing. "I can't believe you have a job that puts you up in places like this."

Georgie flashed a brilliant grin. "Yeah, it's pretty awesome. But I might be moving in a different direction soon."

The doors opened, and Georgie fished the room key out of her back pocket.

"What kind of direction?" She knew from experience that Georgie could go in a million different directions and still land on her feet. "Surgeon? Astronaut? Real estate agent to the stars?"

"Even better. TV show host."

Ashley stopped in her tracks and gaped. "Are you kidding me?"

Georgie laughed and unlocked the door. "Cross my heart. Part of the Ibiza trip was an audition."

"What kind of show? Talk? Cooking? America's Next Top Club Promoter?"

Georgie pulled her into the room and tossed the keycard on the entry table. It was a suite, sunny and spacious. She grabbed two beers from the minifridge and led the way to the balcony. "Come on, let's gab out here."

Ashley waited approximately half a second after her butt hit the chair cushion to start the inquisition. "How did it go? What's the show about? When will you find out? How did this happen?"

Georgie squinted in concentration. "Um, good. Travel for the party set. Approximately thirty seconds before you walked in the lobby. And a friend of a friend of a boss."

"You got it?"

Georgie took a dainty sip from the bottle. "They offered it to me and gave me twenty-four hours to think about it."

"Holy crap. My best friend is going to be on TV."

"Hey, I didn't say yes yet!"

"Are you crazy? Georgie, you couldn't possibly have designed a better job for yourself. You were born to do this!"

"Born to travel and party?" she snorted.

"Don't laugh it off and pretend this isn't your freaking dream. This is an amazing opportunity!"

Georgie broke into a huge grin. "I know! I don't think I let myself know how much I wanted it until I heard that it was mine." She flopped back in her chair and sighed. "Now, tell me about your life. What's going on?"

Ashley took a long, fortifying drink. "Let's just say it's not parties and TV happy. I don't even know where to start. I'm a mess."

"ASAP, how bad could it be? You are a master of disaster. You can see your way through anything."

"Steven's cheating on me with a woman from work. They're both involved with some kind of illegal business deal and their boss and an incredibly hot, devious security expert want me to play spy to help them build a case against him."

Georgie sat in slack-jawed silence.

"Are you okay? Do you need some water or something?" Ashley offered.

Georgie shook her head and only then closed her mouth. "Uhhh. Hmm." She took a hasty swig of her beer. "I don't know what to say. I thought you were going to tell me that you were thinking about breaking your engagement or something."

"Well, I am, obviously."

"Umm...I..."

"I feel like you're taking this worse than I did."

"When did you find out? What's the asshole woman like? I don't know whether to hope that she's hideous-looking or horribly beautiful. Which is better for you? And are you up for spy games? Also, exactly how hot is the devious security expert? Do you have pictures?"

"Last night. Horribly beautiful and I'm not sure which would be worse either. I have no idea how to spy. And, oh-so-incredibly hot. Thank God he's completely ruthless and untrustworthy or I might have let him have his way with me on the racquetball court."

Georgie was gaping at her again. "I think I'm going to call room service for some pizza and more beer and you'd better start from the beginning."

~

"WELL, you don't look like a woman scorned," Georgie said, eyeing Ashley's reflection. "You look like a glamazon who's out to destroy and conquer."

"You don't think it's a bit much...or maybe not enough?" Ashley fingered the hem of the tribal print mini. It peeked out from under the silky black tank with a banded back that revealed a hell of a lot more skin than she was used to. Sky-high strappy sandals wrapped her calves gladiator-style.

Her hair was artfully disheveled in soft, beachy waves courtesy of Georgie's ceramic curling iron. Smokey eye makeup and dark lips gave her a dangerous-looking edge.

They had splurged on mani/pedis in the hotel spa after the beer and pizza. While Georgie had gone for disco ball silver, Ashley went with a metallic black to match her mood.

Georgie joined her in front of the mirror. Her gold-fringed mini dress clung to exactly all the right spots. "Damn, we're hot. Watch out Wilmington."

Ashley laughed and let the feeling push back against the cold, dark knot in her stomach. Tonight was for forgetting about yesterday and not worrying about tomorrow.

LAUNCH, the club, lived up to Georgie's predictions. It was loud, crowded, and dark. The perfect recipe for success on the club scene.

Purple neon glimmered off glass and stainless steel at the bar. The beat of the music hammered in Ashley's head, making it impossible to think about anything. A welcome respite.

Perched on clear acrylic stools at one of the club's three bars, she handed Georgie a shot of tequila. "To us." She raised her glass to her friend's.

"Long may we reign," Georgie yelled over the music.

Ashley knocked back her shot and reached for a lemon slice. "I seem to remember liking these better in college," she wheezed.

Georgie snorted through her lemon. "We were younger and dumber back then."

The bartender set two more shots in front of them.

"To younger and dumber," Ashley toasted.

"Cheers!"

Georgie exhaled tequila fumes and pushed her empty glass to the service bar. "I'm going to go scope out the ladies' room and then see if I can find the shift manager to get some info. Are you okay by yourself for a little while?"

"I'm going to have a nice, delicious ice water and go check out the view from the balcony. Meet you back here?"

"Perfect! Do me a favor and get a pic of the dance floor from upstairs. I want to see how the lights look from above."

"You got it," Ashley said with an exaggerated wink.

Georgie gave her a thumbs-up before disappearing into the crowd.

Ashley flagged the bartender down for a bottle of water, then turned to survey the scene. Between flashes of light from the dance floor, she watched the anonymous bodies writhe together in a wave.

It was a good place to be a stranger.

So why did she feel so vulnerable?

She slid off the barstool and paused to shrug off the happy spin of tequila. The beers from earlier in the evening and two shots could add up to put her close to her no-hangover limit.

She decided to move and hydrate. Ashley made her way around the dance floor toward the stairs that led up to the second level.

A pair of hands preceded by a pungent cologne cloud snaked out of the crowd to grab her hips from behind.

"No thanks." Ashley briskly slapped the hands away and kept walking. She rolled her eyes. There was something about darkness in clubs that made people brave and stupid, like anonymous comments online.

She gingerly took the red-carpeted stairs one at a time. Between the shoes and the booze, she was feeling a little unsteady.

"Hey."

A lifeguard-looking guy with muscles barely restrained by his black t-shirt nodded at her when they passed on the stairs.

"Hey," she nodded back, nonchalantly.

He winked and continued his descent.

Ashley grinned. *See? She could totally do the single thing again. Piece of cake.*

Except the anxiety over first dates. And the bad blind dates. And the fact that she'd be expected to spend every

Friday and Saturday night for the foreseeable future out instead of curled up on the couch in pajama pants.

Damn. There were upsides to long-term monogamous relationships. Just not the one she was currently in. Or pretending to be in. Maybe she should just enjoy being single. No one throwing their vote in on what takeout to order. No one else's schedule to juggle. No one's disgusting hair to pick out of the shower drain.

Huh. That actually sounded pretty good.

Ashley shook her head. Too many thoughts, not enough tequila. She'd snap a picture from the balcony and then find the second-floor bar.

She put her water glass down on a cocktail table next to the railing and fumbled for her phone in her clutch.

The hairs on the back of her neck stood up, and the spot between her shoulder blades tingled. She knew what that meant. *Danger.*

13

*J*ason Baine leaned casually on the other side of the table.

Dressed in another suit—this time sans tie—he had a beer in his hand and an unreadable expression on his perfect face.

They stared at each other in silence for a few seconds until Ashley crossed her arms. "I take it this isn't a coincidence?"

He pulled a phone from his jacket pocket and handed it to her. Georgie's Facebook status was on the screen. "Happy hour(s) with ASAP. Let the tequila flow at Launch!"

"Is there a reason you're stalking me through my Facebook friends? How did you know ASAP was me?"

He raised an eyebrow, and she rolled her eyes. "Right, security expert. I forgot."

"Do you really think it's a good idea for you to be wandering around a club by yourself, half drunk?" His tone was clipped, annoyed. And that annoyed *her*.

She snorted. "I don't see how it's any of your concern."

He rounded the table, stepping between her and the railing.

She frowned up at him. "I'm off the job for tonight, *boss.*"

"I can see that. I'm wondering if you're off the job permanently."

"You're starting to really piss me off." She jutted out her chin. "I don't have to justify to you how I spend my time. I don't have to help you nail my cheating bastard of a soon-to-be-ex-fiancé to a wall either. Lady's choice."

"Holy fireworks." Georgie magically appeared at her side. "I leave you alone for five minutes, and you pick a fight with Tall, Dark, and Angry."

"For you." She handed Ashley one of the cosmos she was carrying and then extended her now empty hand to Jason.

"I'm Georgie, the keeper of this lovely lady tonight."

He took her hand. "Perhaps you should try keeping her a little closer. She was wandering around here alone." Jason's tone was cool. Ashley wondered if he was the one man on the planet immune to Georgie's charm.

"You don't have to be rude, Jason. Georgie, this is Jason the hot, devious security guy. Jason, this is my best friend, Georgie, who knows that I'm completely capable of taking care of myself. Now, if you'll excuse us. We have many more beverages to consume."

She clinked her glass to Georgie's. "Cheers," they said in unison.

Ashley sipped deeply.

"So you're *that* Jason," Georgie said, eyeing him over her glass. "Interesting."

"Hot, devious security guy?" His mouth quirked. "Should I add that to my business cards?"

"Don't take it as a compliment." Ashley frowned. "I'm not feeling very complimentary toward you right now."

Jason smiled, but his phone signaled. Glancing at it, he frowned. "I have to take this. Will you please wait here?"

"See? Why don't you start all of your conversations by being polite? It's so much more pleasant."

Taking that for a yes, he paced away to deal with the phone call.

Georgie smacked her shoulder. "*That* is super hot security guy?"

"Yep." She glumly took a large gulp of cosmo. "And he's not happy that I'm here jeopardizing his plan."

"Did he say that?"

"I don't know. It was more like 'I'm Jason Baine. I'm very tall and angry. You should feel bad. Blah blah blah.'"

Georgie dissolved into a fit of laughter. "Oh my God, I've missed you! Especially drunk you."

"I missed you, too! What am I going to do while you're off gallivanting all over the world?"

"Gallivanting? That's a lot of syllables for someone in your condition."

They were still laughing when Jason returned, stowing his phone in his jacket pocket. "Ladies, I would like to apologize for getting off on the wrong foot. Can we start over? And may I join you?"

"Please excuse me while I confer with my colleague," Ashley said snootily.

The two women turned their backs on him and began whispering. They nodded and turned as one to face him.

"Your apology will be accepted, and you will be allowed to join us if you meet the following criteria," Ashley announced.

"One, you will take a picture of us because, let's face it, we look awesome and our arms aren't long enough to capture the head-to-toe awesome in a selfie," Georgie said.

"And two, you will go to the bartender and order a strawberry daiquiri with extra whipped cream, which you will then drink," Ashley said, crossing her arms. "Do you accept these terms?"

Jason bit back a sigh. "Give me your phone."

~

HE WAS A SURPRISINGLY GOOD SPORT, Ashley thought, hand under her chin, as she watched Jason suck down the last of his daiquiri.

"Good?"

"It's actually not bad." He gazed into the glass, frowning.

"Just wait until the sugar rush hits you," Georgie warned. "If you drink more than one of those an hour you might end up in a diabetic coma."

He pushed the glass away. "Good to know. So, now what?"

"Now, we dance!" Georgie pushed back from the table. "We finally have a bodyguard, ASAP!"

Ashley laughed. "It's nice to have a guy on the floor or lurking nearby so strangers don't get too, um, handsy," she explained. She pulled him with her as she followed Georgie toward the stairs.

"Are you a dancer or a lurker?" she asked over her shoulder as they descended.

"What?"

The music was pulsing at brain-vibrating levels.

She stopped suddenly on the last step, and Jason gripped her shoulders to steady her. She leaned back against him. The alcohol made him slightly less scary and unfortunately even more...desirable.

"I said, are you a dancer or a lurker?"

"Let's find out."

She caught up with Georgie, and together they wound their way through the bodies on the floor to the center.

She noted that Jason had stationed himself at the bar. Lurking.

"Looks like your friend can't hang," Georgie shouted over the music.

Ashley shook her head and relaxed into the music. "I'm not surprised. No one can look that good in a suit *and* dance."

"Are you going to sleep with him?"

Ashley tripped over her feet. "What?"

Georgie leaned in. "You heard me! Are you?"

"Oh my God, Georgie!"

"Oh my God is right!" Swaying to the music, she ticked points off on her fingers. "He's gorgeous. He knows your engagement is non-existent. He cares enough to stalk you to a club and babysit you. And he can't take his eyes off of you."

Ashley shot a peek in his direction. And met his gaze.

"Ash, he *smolders.*"

He really did. "But I can't just sleep with him. I haven't even gotten out of the relationship I'm in."

"Steven has already exited the relationship. You're not in a relationship. You just have a shitty roommate."

"I know that!" Ashley's voice battled the music. "But look at him."

They both turned to study Jason as he gave a hopeful, boobalicious brunette the brush off. "How would I hold my own? I get overwhelmed just having a conversation with him. And I already know I can't trust him."

"There are some men you don't have to hold your own with. You just be you, let him be him, and enjoy this gift from God to make up for the shitstorm you're in now."

"So you're saying I'd be stupid not to?"

"Never stupid, my lovely friend. Just chicken."

"Bawk. Bawk. I'm just not ready yet. And I don't know if I'll ever be ready for someone as smolder-y as Jason Baine."

"I choose to respectfully disagree, but still support your decision," Georgie sighed.

"That's fair of you."

The song changed, and Georgie squealed. "I love this song!" A man in a pink fedora caught her eye. "You in the hat," she bellowed.

Ashley laughed and watched Georgie and her new friend weave and slide in a complicated step.

She threw her hands up and swayed to the beat. Music therapy.

Hands slid around her waist from behind. But they weren't the right hands. Sweaty palms and thick fingers squeezed her hips.

She stepped out of the grip and turned. Her uninvited partner was no Jason Baine. A few sheets to the wind and barely taller than she was, he was glistening under a beady layer of sweat.

When he reached for her again, she shook her head. "No thanks."

"Come on, baby." He made a grab for her arm, and she side-stepped him.

"Still no."

Another pair of hands settled on her hips. The right ones.

She felt the energy and the heat slide through her.

"Leave. Now." Jason didn't have to shout over the music. The message was received loud and clear, and her sweaty friend beat a hasty retreat.

Jason turned her around and pulled her in close. After the shortest hesitation, she brought her arms around his neck. Even in her heels, she had to lean her head back to look at him.

They moved together to the beat. His hands roamed her back, and she enjoyed the shiver of skin on skin contact.

"Thank you, but it wasn't necessary."

"I'm sure you can take care of yourself, but I thought I would streamline the process."

"I appreciate the thought."

"When I see you make dangerous choices, it worries me."

"I'm not going to jeopardize your secret mission. It's just a night out with my friend."

"I'm not concerned with the 'mission.' I'm worried about you. I want you to be safe."

"Why should you care when my own fiancé doesn't?"

"I care about what happens to you." He reached out and traced her jawline with his finger.

She felt the blush warm her cheeks. Her bare knees brushed the inside of his pant legs.

"I don't know what to say to that. What I do with my time isn't really your concern."

"And yet it still concerns me."

"So where does that leave us?"

"In a strange situation." This time he ran the pad of his thumb over her lower lip. She considered it a victory when she didn't let it tremble.

Her lips parted, and she touched her tongue to his skin for just a second. She saw the change in his eyes. The sharpening. He pulled her tighter against him, trailing his hand down her jaw to her neck.

"Guys!"

Ashley guiltily jumped back and into Georgie. They tangled and almost went down in a heap before Jason reached out to steady them.

"I can see it's time for another round of drinks," he said wryly.

"Let's make it a last call round," Georgie suggested. "I've

got a family breakfast tomorrow. Gramps hates when I show up hungover."

He gave Ashley's arm a squeeze. "I'll get the drinks." He disappeared into the crowd.

"What was *that*?" She smacked Georgie's arm.

Georgie smacked her back. "What was what?"

"I was going to kiss him. I was in the process of getting ready to kiss him, and you interrupted on purpose!"

"Uh, yeah! He looked like he was going to eat you alive after you just got done telling me you weren't ready."

"Didn't you just get done telling me to be ready?"

"I am trying to be respectful of my friend's questionable life choices."

Ashley groaned. "Thanks. I think."

"How about a compromise? Sleep on it tonight before deciding whether or not you're a giant chicken depriving herself of..." She glanced over her shoulder to where Jason stood at the bar. "What could be one of life's finest pleasures."

Ashley followed her gaze. "Do you think we're building this up to be some ridiculous fantasy that reality could never live up to?"

"Nope. Most epic sex ever."

Ashley sighed. "Yeah, that's what I thought."

THEY DID THEIR FINAL SHOTS, and Jason carefully packed them into a cab and sent them back to Georgie's hotel, but not before making her promise she would text when they got into the room.

Ashley didn't bother asking him how he knew where she was staying. She was too busy holding the hand he had kissed to her mouth as she gazed out the window.

"You're spending the night, right?" Georgie demanded on a yawn.

"I can't let you enjoy that amazing hotel suite all by yourself, now can I?"

She felt warm and sleepy and...cared for. It wasn't so bad.

"Awesome," Georgie said in a sing-song voice.

14

A whistling Steven woke Ashley from a reasonably erotic dream about Jason.

"Babe. Wake up. Are you coming?"

She was just about to in the dream, before the unfortunate interruption.

"Mmmmph," she mumbled into her pillow. She wasn't prepared to give up the dream and face her reality. Georgie's alarm had gone off at 6:30 that morning, and Ashley decided to do the walk of shame home rather than staying until check out. She had crawled into bed just after seven to catch a few more hours of sleep.

"Come on, babe. Blueberry pancakes? Bacon? Lots of coffee?"

She rolled onto her side. "Brunch?" What had once been a weekly tradition for them had fizzled this year into a some-thing they "used to do."

"Yeah. I haven't seen much of you lately and my tee time's not until 1. Come on, it'll be like old times."

Not likely, Ashley thought. Old times didn't involve him sticking his dick in other women. Or had they?

She was torn. The last thing she wanted to do was spend a leisurely Sunday morning meal with Steven. But what better way to get information than from the stupid horse's mouth?

She sighed into her pillow. "Give me ten minutes, and I'll be ready." She waited until she heard him leave before dragging herself out of bed to pull on clean yoga pants and a soft long-sleeve tee in royal blue. She piled her hair on her head in a messy knot, added a coat of mascara to her lashes, and layered a scarf around her neck.

She found Steven in the living room dressed in khaki pants and a polo shirt. He quickly slid his phone in his pocket when he spotted her. It was something he had done a million times before, only now she knew what it meant.

When had her common sense completely abandoned her?

The signs were so obvious now that she was even angrier with herself for not picking up on it on her own. It took a mega-millionaire with a racquetball court to point out the painfully obvious.

She pasted a smile on her face. "Ready to go?"

"Is that what you're wearing?" He eyed her outfit critically.

Two days ago that judgment would have sent her hustling back to the closet.

"Yep." She breezed past him, grabbing her wallet and phone off of the kitchen island. "Let's go."

Normally she would argue that they should walk the four blocks to Randolph House, but today with a dull headache and a new reason to avoid fights, she just hid behind oversized sunglasses and slid into the passenger seat.

"So who's golfing today?" Pretending like she had shits left to give. She settled back against the leather seat and let Steven ramble on about his foursome.

～

ASHLEY TOOK a bite of bacon and looked at Steven. Really looked at him. His light hair was getting a little long. There was a slight curl to the ends, which usually signaled a haircut was on the schedule.

His shirt was neatly pressed, and she wondered if he had taken up ironing or if he had just decided to start having all his clothing dry-cleaned. He was wearing a watch that she had never seen before. A very nice watch.

"Nice watch," she said, gesturing with the bacon at the flashy unit on his wrist.

He glanced down at it and adjusted the band on his wrist. "Thanks. It's new."

"Can I see it?"

He extended his arm, and she pulled his hand closer. It was the first time she had voluntarily touched him since she found out. She tried not to think about how much she wanted to snap his forearm in half and instead studied the watch face.

It was a Rolex.

"I thought I'd treat myself to something new."

He thought he would treat himself to a Rolex? There was no way in hell he could afford a brand-new Rolex. "It's, uh, really nice."

He pulled his arm back and took a gulp of orange juice. "Thanks. I figured since things are going well, I deserved something nice."

The guy who borrowed $20 off of her last week to pay the pizza delivery guy deserved a gold fucking Rolex?

She was willing to bet that the watch came from a certain ice-cold blonde. Maybe it was a "thanks for breaking the law and cheating on your fiancée with me" gift. A double punch in the gut since Ashley had saved for months to buy him his last watch for graduation. At the time, a $500 watch had seemed like a priceless treasure.

She bit her tongue and focused on her omelet.

"So what's happening at work these days? Are you still looking at other options?"

Oblivious, Steven carved up his sausage with enthusiasm. "Yeah, I'm looking at a couple of opportunities. One in particular."

"Is it in the city?"

"Initially, but there's a possibility of relocation."

Ashley just stared at him. "Uh-huh." A hundred snarky comments ran through her mind. The guy was thinking of picking up and moving and hadn't thought to mention it to her? The woman he was supposed to marry? No thought given to her job, her life here in the city. *Weasel-faced douchebag.*

Maybe he was planning on moving with someone else.

She took a deep, quiet breath. "Is there a timeline on that? Do you know when the offer will come through?"

"Couple of weeks. Probably by the end of next month."

Her fork slipped out of her hand and clattered on the plate.

"Wow, that's soon," she cleared her throat and reached for her coffee.

He shrugged as he plowed his way through his pancakes. "It's time for a change, don't you think?"

"I couldn't agree more."

The waitress had cleared their plates and was returning with the check when Steven's phone rang. He glanced at the screen and hastily stood up.

"I gotta take this, babe. Do you mind getting the check?" He turned and headed toward the bar without waiting for an answer. "Hey, yeah. No, it's not a bad time."

Ashley rolled her eyes and reached for her wallet. Her phone signaled on the table.

Jason: You looked beautiful last night. How are you feeling?

She couldn't stop the smile or the warm feeling in her chest as she read Jason's text. Damn it. She was probably going to sleep with him. And it was probably going to be amazing.

15

*S*ince she had the rest of her Sunday free, Ashley decided to change and go into the store for a few hours to get a head start on the next week's paperwork.

The more she got done now, the more time she could devote to stalking Steven while he was at work. The store was only open until 3, so she could keep Janice company for a bit before hibernating in the back office.

Dressed in slim black capris and a simple black boatneck sweater, she deemed herself respectable enough for customers and comfortable enough for any bending and lifting that might be required.

She found Janice helping the very pregnant Magda Olson, a vascular surgeon with impeccable taste, with her purchases.

"Dr. Olson! You look wonderful! How much longer?" Ashley asked, pointing at the baby bump.

"Two more weeks! Janice was just showing me these watercolor prints. What do you think of them for the nursery?"

Ashley eyed the dreamy seascapes with their slashes of greens and blues. "Do you still have the picture of the nursery on your phone?"

"Of course! Why didn't I think of that? Ugh, baby brain. Here it is!" Triumphantly, she pulled her phone from the depths of her leather tote and swiped through her pictures. "Aha!"

Ashley glanced at the screen and back again at the prints. "Dr. Olson, these are perfect! It's like they were painted for your room."

Dr. Olson did a little shimmy. "Wrap 'em up, ladies! The nursery is officially done."

Laughing, Janice led the doctor to the register while Ashley stayed behind to rearrange the display. The inventory on the prints was getting a little low, and she made a mental note to reach out to the artist to see if he had anything else ready for them.

She spent the next hour helping out with a handful of customers before heading back to the office.

She emailed the watercolor artist while it was still fresh in her mind and then opened up the financials. The past month had seemed busier than usual, and she wanted to see if the figures agreed.

Barbara would be very pleased, Ashley thought as she worked her way through the weeks. They were already over last year's total for the month, and there was still two weeks left.

They were probably ready to hire another part-time staffer to help cover the weekends, especially with summer on the way. She was writing up an employment ad to send to Barbara for approval when the desk phone rang.

"What's up?"

"Yes, I was just checking to see if Mr. Donahue's order was in yet?" Janice's voice was breezy and professional, but Ashley could hear the smile in it.

She laughed into the receiver. "Mr. Donahue" was code for "come out and see something funny/sexy/weird."

"On my way!" Ashley hung up and hurried out.

The last time there was a Mr. Donahue, it was a woman with two tiny Yorkies in matching argyle sweaters in matching Louis Vuitton bags.

She headed straight for Janice behind the register. "What is it?" she whispered. Janice didn't take her eyes off the front of the store but nodded in that direction.

It wasn't a tiny dog. It was a tall man in an impeccable suit. *Jason.*

Ashley tried to ignore the butterflies that instantly took flight.

"I asked him if I could help him find anything, but he said he was just looking. Would you mind if I eloped with him and took a few weeks off from work for a honeymoon full of orgasms and champagne?"

"Go right ahead, but let me talk to your groom first."

Janice fanned herself with a brochure. "Don't get too close. You might get singed."

"You're not kidding," Ashley said under her breath. She left the safety of the counter and crossed to him. Even on a Sunday, he was in a suit. Today's was a crisp navy with subtle gray pinstripes.

He turned toward her as if sensing her. "Hello."

What was it about that voice? Like whiskey by firelight.

"Hi. What are you doing here?" She kept her tone low and busied her hands by rearranging the soy candle display.

"I was in the neighborhood before a meeting and found myself in need of a gift."

"And so you came here?"

"It came highly recommended by the manager."

She smiled wryly. "She sounds very smart. What kind of

gift? Who is the lucky recipient? And is it safe for us to be seen together?"

"So many questions." Jason picked up a sandalwood candle and sniffed. "Something shiny and fussy for a woman who has been my right hand for nine years. And as long as you can control yourself and not tear my clothes off, we should be fine."

She rolled her eyes. "I'll try to keep my baser instincts at bay," she said dryly.

She noticed Janice across the store performing an exaggerated fanning motion from behind the counter.

"Why don't we look over here?" Ashley pointed toward the far side of the store, out of Janice's line of sight.

She guided them around the divider wall currently used as gallery space for black and white scenes of the River Walk.

Jason glanced around at the corner displays. "This must be your shiny and fussy section."

Vibrant candleholders, glittery napkin rings, small tile-framed mirrors, and hand-painted barware mingled on shelves and tabletops in a riot of color and shine.

"I don't know where to look first," he said.

Ashley laughed. "That's usually what men say when they visit this part of the store. Tell me more about your right hand."

"Her name is Mona. She'll be 59 on Monday, she gives her annual bonus to her favorite animal shelter, enjoys cheap wine in crystal glasses, and sponsors a high school student at a local art camp every summer. And if she ever retires I'll be lost without her."

Ashley clasped her hands together. "She sounds wonderful. I think I have the perfect thing." She moved to a primitive hutch and gently lifted a glass vase from the shelf. "This is a hand-blown bell vase made out of recycled glass. It was made by a woman in Swaziland. In Africa. Her village collects glass bottles, and she turns them into treasures."

Jason took the vase from her and held it up to the light. It was heavy, but with flowing fluted curves that were almost sensual. The flecks of bubbles beneath the surface gave the piece charm.

"Perfect. Now what do we put in it?"

"Calla lilies. Pink," she said with a nod. "We work with a florist on the next block over who does beautiful arrangements. I have his card at the register."

"You're very good at this."

"Thank you. We take finding the perfect gift pretty seriously here."

He handed the vase back to her. "How do you feel today?" He kept his voice low, his eyes on her face.

Standing so close with fingers touching on the cool glass, she felt the goose bumps rise on her skin.

Too many complications. Keep it simple, she ordered herself.

"I have a little headache, but that's more from brunch than last night."

"Did you both survive brunch?"

"Barely. He's wearing a new Rolex, which I think might be a gift. And he's expecting a job offer by the end of next month."

Jason nodded and mulled over the information. "So it sounds like our timeline just got tighter. Have dinner with me tonight. We can discuss what I need you to look for."

She raised an eyebrow. "Dinner? Why not just text me?"

He smiled and pushed a strand of hair behind her ear. "You have to eat, don't you? Consider this multi-tasking."

"Hmm." She tapped a finger to her chin. "I guess it all comes down to where we're going for dinner."

"My house?"

"Nice try, champ. No."

He sighed. "Fine. I'll take you out. In public. Where you can't maul me."

She nodded. "Then I accept your invitation."

He grinned. "I thought you might. It's hard to resist a hot, devious security guy."

She rolled her eyes. "I knew that one would come back to bite me. You're lucky my only other dinner option is with Steven, and one meal with him was enough. Especially when I had to pick up the check while he took a call from his girlfriend."

"Remember, my shovel is at your disposal. Just try not to need it until we have enough to nail them to a wall." He glanced discreetly at his watch. "Do you mind ringing me up before I go? I can pick you up back here at six."

She felt a little tickle of disappointment and immediately quashed it. She didn't like that there was something electric about being close to him. Her heart beat a little faster, and her senses were a bit sharper when he was in the room. But maybe that was because she still felt like a mouse in the presence of a mountain lion around him.

Simple. Simple, simple, simple.

"Sure," she smiled brightly. "We do very nice gift wrapping, but if you're going to get Mona the flowers it would make more of a statement if it was all put together on her desk when she comes in on Monday."

"Good point."

She led him back to the register...and Janice.

"Janice, this is Mr. Baine."

Janice gave him a dazzling smile. "Good afternoon, Mr. Baine. You have excellent taste," she nodded at the vase.

"Thank you, Janice. I just went with the expert's opinion."

"That's usually the safest bet around here." She laughed. "And what will be going in it?"

"Calla lilies," Ashley said, as she peeled off the discreet price tag.

"Pink," Jason supplied.

Janice nodded her approval and nudged Ashley with her foot.

"Janice, could you give Mr. Baine Lorenzo's card?" She punctuated her request by stepping on Janice's foot.

"Certainly," she chirped. "Lorenzo is a wonderful florist, Mr. Baine."

Ashley gave Jason the total, noting that the amount—high enough to purchase a very respectable pair of Ferragamos—didn't even warrant a blink.

He scrawled his signature across the receipt and handed the pen back to her, fingers lingering. "Thank you for your help."

She tried to ignore the humming in her ears as their gazes held and fingers brushed.

He strolled to the door leaving, Ashley and Janice watching him.

"Who was that? How do you know him? And how did you not melt into a puddle just now?"

Ashley blew out a breath and braced herself against the counter. "So it's not just me? He's really that intensely hot?"

"I have traveled all over this world and dated many, many, *many* handsome men. And I can say definitively that that is the hottest man on the planet. I repeat, how do you know him?"

"I met him at some cocktail party Friday night for Steven's work."

"You met him Friday, and he showed up here today? He is

clearly into you. What does Steven say? Oh, screw Steven. Put him next to Mr. Hot Body and he looks like a garden gnome."

Ashley snorted in spite of herself. Janice's opinion of Steven hadn't been very high since he stood Ashley up on Valentine's Day last year. He went for drinks after work and didn't make it home until the next morning.

She thought about explaining the situation to Janice but decided against it. The fewer people who knew what was going on, the better it would be. And the faster it could be over.

∼

ASHLEY CLOSED the office door and leaned against it. She wished she could shut everything out of her mind as easily.

Anger over Steven and his infidelity warred with too many thoughts about Jason. She didn't know what was happening there, but she was entirely too preoccupied with him. Visions crowded her mind. His face, those piercing eyes, the feeling she got when she found him watching her.

She shook her head to clear it. The absolute last thing she needed in her life right now was some overblown infatuation, she cautioned herself. *She was going to be single, keep things simple.*

"There is no room in your life for someone like Jason Baine," she reminded herself. His presence was too big, too powerful. She could lose herself there.

Maybe dinner tonight was a bad idea.

Her phone on the desk buzzed.

Steven: Won't be home for dinner. Late meeting.

She was pretty sure she knew what kind of a late meeting

Steven would be having on a Sunday. It made her skin crawl. How many times had he touched her after coming home from being with Victoria? She wanted to throw up or set something on fire.

Well, now there was no reason not to go to dinner with Jason.

"It's just dinner," she whispered.

She could keep a safe distance from Jason no matter what happened physically *and* cut Steven out of her life. A clean break and a fresh start. That was exactly what she needed.

16
---

*A*shley left the store to run some errands after closing. She caught the tail end of the farmer's market and stocked up on a few things for lunches at the store. Then she hit the drugstore to pick up a prescription and ended up buying half of the cosmetics aisle to spice up her look before "just dinner." There wasn't enough time to run home to change clothes, but at least her face could look fancier.

"It's just dinner, it's no big deal," she chanted, applying a rosy shade to her lips and smudged eyeliner into her lash line.

She returned to the store floor to finish unpacking a small delivery and add the new items to the sales system. The display of hand-painted dishes was taking shape, and she was sure pieces would be walking out the door starting Monday morning.

Startled by a knock on the glass, she turned and took a deep breath. Jason was at the door. Waiting.

Ashley unlocked the door and held it open for him. He was still in his suit, and she felt a little self-conscious about her clothing choice. "We're not going anywhere fancy, are we?" She glanced down at her outfit and ballet flats.

He slid his hands in pockets. "You're more than fine."

"We look like we're going to two different dinners."

Jason studied her for a beat and then loosened his tie. He pulled it off, stuffed it into his jacket pocket, then undid the top button of his crisp white shirt.

"Better?"

Ashley couldn't help but stare at the hint of skin. "Much."

He glanced around the darkened store. "Do you need to do anything before we go?"

She locked the front door. "Let me grab my bag and arm the alarm. We can go out the back." She led the way past the register and down the hallway to the office. He waited in the doorway, making the tiny space feel even more crowded. She tossed her phone into the clutch and switched off the desk lamp, sending the room into darkness. Fumbling for the keys, she turned and ran solidly into him.

He steadied her with his hands, his face shrouded in darkness. The only illumination was the red glow behind him from the dull exit sign in the hallway.

She could feel his breath on her upturned face. Her pulse quickened. He was so close. The heat pumping off of his body warmed her palms through his shirt. He smelled like soap and spices.

"Why do we keep ending up here?" she asked softly.

"You know why." His mouth was just a whisper away from her lips. His long fingers flexed their grip on her arms.

She could hear her blood pumping in her head. "Don't you think this is a really stupid idea?"

His breath was hot on her skin. "Yes, it is." He released her arms but captured her hand when she started to step back. Jason turned it palm up and lowered his lips to the center. "I want to see you when I touch you the first time."

Ashley's fingers went lax, and her clutch plummeted to the

floor. Her palm tingled from his kiss, and she knew with certainty that's how every inch of her body would react to those perfect lips.

She jerked her hand away and stepped back. "The darkness isn't the stupid idea I was referring to," she said dryly.

Jason stood with his arms crossed. In silhouette, he was even more intimidating.

She switched the lamp back on. Now she could see rather than just feel the intensity of his gaze.

"Do you really think that us hooking up when I'm supposed to be helping you spy on my fiancé is a good idea?"

"Are you that afraid of me that you think one little kiss would end in catastrophe?" he countered.

"Yes."

Jason laughed.

"And don't think for one second that I believe that it would be 'one little kiss.' I don't know what this is." She gestured between them. "But I know it's something. You're aware of it, too. And we both know it's got disaster written all over it."

"Let's agree to disagree." He put his palms up when she started to argue. "Come on. Let's go. I'm hungry."

She snatched her clutch off the floor and snapped off the light. "Come on, Romeo."

He watched her double-check that the exit door bar was locked before she entered the code in the ancient keypad. Once outside in the alley, she leaned heavily against the door and then tested the handle.

He ran his fingers over gouge marks dug into the doorframe.

"We had a break in last year," Ashley explained.

"Do you always leave through the back?"

She stashed her keys in her bag and nodded. "There's only

twenty seconds between setting the alarm and it arming, so it's not enough time to make it back to the front of the store."

"There's not a lot of light back here," he noted, glancing around the alley as they walked toward the next cross street.

"It's fine this time of year. It's mostly daylight when we close."

"Where do you park?"

"In the garage two blocks over. Barbara, the owner, got us all cans of mace and little LED flashlights for when we close after dark."

He said nothing. He walked shoulder to shoulder with her, hands in his pockets again.

"Is the big, bad security expert judging our setup?" she teased.

"There's always room for improvement."

They rounded the corner onto the side street and turned again into the hustle and bustle of storefronts, restaurants, and the Sunday evening crowd. Jason guided her, a hand at the small of her back, toward a sleek, black sedan parked at the curb. She goggled at the emblem on the hood.

"Is this a freaking Tesla?"

He laughed. "Yes. This is a freaking Tesla." He opened the passenger door for her, and she slid onto the two-tone leather seat.

"Quick question. Do you mind if I make out with your car?" she asked when he settled behind the wheel.

"No, but you might have more fun driving it."

"Don't tease me about driving a Tesla, Jason."

He grinned. "We'll see how dinner goes." He started the nearly silent engine and smoothly pulled away from the curb.

"So, where are we going? I'm not up on my spy etiquette. Is it safe to be seen together?"

"Given the situation, I thought it would be smarter to keep a low profile."

A non-answer. How typically annoying.

Ashley leaned back against her seat to enjoy the ride. Forty-eight hours ago her life had been on a completely different path. And now? Now she was cruising out of Wilmington in a Tesla toward the unknown with a man she'd just met. One she was fairly certain she couldn't trust.

They headed north, the coast unwinding on their right in the slanting evening light. The silence between them was heavy, but neither tried to break it.

The city was far behind them when Jason pulled into the gravel lot of a cozy beachfront café.

"Do you like seafood?" he asked.

"Almost as much as I like racquetball."

17

The hostess, a runway model of a brunette, led them to a quiet table on the deck overlooking the ocean and hovered for a moment too long while Jason pulled out Ashley's chair. Ashley couldn't blame the girl. Jason Baine wasn't just easy on the eyes, he demanded their full attention.

He shed his jacket and hung it on the back of his chair. When he sat, he unbuttoned his cuffs and worked at rolling up his sleeves.

"I feel like I'm watching Jason the mogul morph into Jason the human being."

He raised an eyebrow and adjusted a cuff. "Like Dr. Jekyll and Mr. Hyde?"

"I'll let you know after dinner."

"Fair enough."

Their waiter, a gangly hipster, arrived with a pitcher of ice water and a plate of freshly baked rosemary bread. He pushed his black-rimmed glasses up his nose as he recited the specials with gusto.

She settled on a glass of white wine and the shrimp and

asparagus special. While Jason ordered, Ashley amused herself with the dessert menu.

"Did you have a good meeting?" she asked when the waiter left them.

"A productive one." He drizzled olive oil over a slice of bread and dropped it neatly on her plate.

"Is that the same thing as good?" Suddenly aware of the lunch she had skipped, she sampled the bread and sighed. "Oh my God, that's delicious."

He raised an eyebrow and helped himself to a slice. "Damn. That is good. And yes, the meeting went well."

"I can imagine you have some interesting meetings on Sunday afternoons in your field."

"Almost as interesting as the ones that take place at three in the morning. Security threats never sleep."

"I assume neither do the people trying to prevent them."

The waiter returned with their drinks.

"How was your day?" he asked.

She blinked over her wineglass. *When was the last time a man had asked her that over dinner?*

"It had its ups and downs."

"Which one is this?" he asked.

"I'm withholding judgment until the shrimp gets here, but so far consider yourself an up."

"How were things at home?"

Ashley leaned back in her chair and toyed with the base of her wineglass. "Hard."

"I can imagine."

"Can you? Have you ever lived with someone whose utter disregard for your feelings suddenly became so clear you felt like an idiot for not seeing it sooner?"

"Yes, but that's not why we're here, Ashley."

Ashley leaned forward and cupped her chin in her hands. "Why don't you tell me why we're here?"

"I need your help."

"You seem to have a lot of resources at your disposal. Why exactly do you need me?"

Jason paused as if weighing his words carefully. "You can get closer to certain information than I can."

"Information that you think Steven has."

Jason nodded.

"And you think he'll be an easier target than Victoria."

"I know he will be."

"So through Steven, you're hoping to get to Victoria."

"Yes."

Ashley took a gulp of wine. She hated putting those two names together in a sentence. A flash of them wrapped around each other on Jason's security monitor sliced through her.

"You're sure what they're doing is illegal?"

"I can't prove anything yet. But yes, I'm sure."

"What's the end game here? What happens if I help you and we find the proof you need?"

"I'll take what we have to the client—in this case, my grandfather. And he will decide whether or not to go to the authorities."

"Who are?"

"For something like insider trading? The SEC and the FBI."

Ashley froze with her glass halfway to her lips. Depending on his involvement, Steven could end up in jail. Like *prison* jail. She was equal parts thrilled and horrified.

"I'm all for karma, but I'm not sure I'm comfortable being a tool of karma."

Jason reached across the table and took her hand. "They're breaking the law. And they obviously aren't earning humanitarian awards in their personal lives either. They're greedy and selfish and careless."

She stayed quiet, stomach and mind churning in unison.

"What information are you looking for? And how do I get it?"

He squeezed her hand before letting go. "We've already forensically imaged his work laptop."

"Did you find anything?"

"A few things. Mostly just a ridiculous amount of porn."

She slammed her glass down.

He continued smoothly. "Ideally, we want to get access to his home computer and his cell phone. However, we can't do that without going to the authorities first. And we can't go to the authorities without proof. That's where you come in."

"You want me to do some good old-fashioned spying—following him, 'accidentally' reading his emails, checking his browser history—so you can get enough to get a warrant."

"Essentially anything that a woman who suspects her significant other of cheating would do."

"Well, that shouldn't be hard." Ashley sighed. "What am I looking for?"

He took a sip of his beer. "Any kind of business communications with someone outside the company. New friends on Facebook, phone numbers that show up on his cell bill repeatedly. I'll get you access to his work calendar so you'll know what are legitimate meetings and what might be happening off the books."

Any further comment was postponed by the arrival of their waiter, dinners in hand. He fussed over their plates for a moment before retreating to the kitchen.

"Enough shop talk," Jason said, leaning forward. "It's a beautiful night, let's enjoy it."

Ashley raised her glass. "To a beautiful night."

He leaned forward and touched his glass to hers. "To us."

"Go, team," she said dryly and dug into her shrimp.

18

———

The strings of lights came on over their heads as daylight shifted to dusk. The patio heaters and outdoor fireplace gave off a comfortable blanket of warmth to chase off the chill.

They lingered over coffee and shared a piece of peanut butter pie, enjoying the ocean view. "After Friday, I didn't think I'd ever feel anything but angry again. And yet here I am licking chocolate syrup off my plate." She ran her finger across the remains of an artful swirl and popped it into her mouth. "Yum."

Jason was watching her. "How do you feel now?"

She was still angry. She was still attracted to Jason. And she still didn't trust him. Either she was already gun-shy or there was something there that she just wasn't seeing yet. Overall, the edge of adrenaline that fury gave her had faded, leaving her drained.

"Tired," she sighed.

"That's understandable." His gaze held.

"I can't tell what you're thinking and I feel like I should."

"Do you really want to know what I'm thinking?"

"I may regret this, but yes."

"I'm thinking that Steven is an idiot."

She sighed and quietly savored the last sip of her wine.

The dishes were cleared, and the restaurant was slowly emptying when their waiter approached with the bill.

"Folks, if you're not in a hurry, we're doing a little bonfire down by the water." He pointed to the beach where there was already a handful of diners and staff clustered around the beginnings of a fire.

"Do you have time?" Jason eyed her across the table.

She raised her eyebrows. "Don't be ridiculous. There's always time for a beach bonfire."

He opened his wallet and handed over a credit card. "Put a bottle of what the lovely lady is drinking on the bill, and we'll take it with us."

"Certainly, sir!"

Wine and plastic cups in hand, they wandered off the deck and down the wooden stairs to the sand. They took off their shoes as the other guests had and walked down the path that cut through the dunes. The night's cool, salty air teased goose bumps onto her skin. She rubbed her arms to ward off the chill. Jason draped an arm over her shoulders and pulled her into his side.

She welcomed the warmth as they walked.

The dunes gave way to a sandy beach with a throng of locals loosely ringing the now crackling bonfire.

Jason steered her closer and set the wine down in the sand. He turned her to face the fire. Ashley closed her eyes and let herself enjoy the heat surrounding her. Flames to the front and a smoldering man behind her. Was there a better place to be?

Safer, yes. But better?

He draped his jacket over her shoulders.

"Better?"

Ashley nodded and snuggled deeper into the jacket. She knew she was being seduced. And she knew she should put a stop to it. But knowing didn't always translate to doing.

"The stars are coming out," he said quietly.

She followed his gaze to the inky blue night sky, dotted with hundreds of pinpoints of light.

"Wow."

"Yeah."

She turned toward him and stopped. He wasn't looking at the sky. He was watching her.

She moved away. Self-preservation, she thought. "It looks like we get dinner and a show."

Off the clock now, their waiter had joined the small group with guitar in hand and the willowy hostess in tow.

They plopped down on a log near the fire. When he started quietly strumming, she dropped her head to his shoulder and wiggled closer.

"Now *that* surprises me," Jason laughed.

"Oh, not me. Even without the bad boy part of the image, 'musician' still carries a lot of weight."

Ashley sank down on a makeshift bench of driftwood and stretched her legs out toward the fire.

Jason retrieved the wine and joined her. She pulled his jacket a little tighter around her. Expertly, he pulled the cork from the bottle and poured.

"Did you ever date a musician?"

She sighed. "No. But I wanted to. Or an artist."

He handed her a cup. "Why not an accountant or a podiatrist?"

"An accountant isn't going to be so overwhelmed with passion for you that he has to capture your essence in a painting or a song."

"'Capture your essence?' You've put a lot of thought into this," he teased.

"It's a girl thing. We are excellent at fantasy."

The waiter's chords slowly turned into a loose, acoustic version of "Louie Louie."

Ashley hummed along. Others around them whispered quietly in cozy twosomes or laughed in small groups.

"Thank you for dinner, Jason."

"My pleasure." He glanced toward the sky again. "I know what I'm asking you to do isn't easy."

"Well, if it weren't for you, I might not even know that I'm engaged to a liar and a cheater."

"I don't know if I should say 'I'm sorry' or 'You're welcome.'"

"Both seem appropriate."

"It's going to be okay, Ashley. I promise you."

She nodded. It would be. Somehow.

They sat in silence for a few minutes. Surrounded by the sounds of fire and waves. The wine slowly eased the tension out of her body.

Ashley caught the first few chords of "Moon River."

"I love this song. It always makes me think of Audrey Hepburn on the fire escape."

"What was she doing on the fire escape?"

"You've never seen *Breakfast at Tiffany's*?" Aghast, she clapped her hands to her heart. "You poor, deprived man."

"How about a dance with a poor, deprived man?" He stood, gracefully, and held out a hand to her.

She glanced around. What the hell? When else was she going to get the chance to dance to "Moon River" barefoot on a beach with a man as intoxicating as Jason? She put her hand in his and let him pull her to her feet.

His arm slid around her waist, pulling her close. Ashley let herself melt against him. Solid, warm, strong. His hand splayed across her back, not allowing an inch of freedom between their bodies.

Somewhere down the beach a fireworks show was starting. She saw an orange starburst join the stars in the sky before shimmering back down to earth.

"This is our second dance. Practically our second date," he said quietly as he tilted his head down toward hers. An invitation.

"What's your game?" she breathed, studying his eyes.

"Why does there have to be a game?"

"I can't read you. You're so...guarded. I'm not used to having to guess how someone is feeling."

"There's no game." He stopped the gentle sway of their bodies, holding her solidly against him. "And this is what I'm feeling." He lowered his mouth in an achingly slow pursuit.

She had time to stop him. To play it safe. But she wanted to know what it would feel like. Just once. To be the object of his desire. To have this first kiss.

Her eyes fluttered shut, and she drew in his breath as his lips met hers. Jason closed his hand around her neck, his thumb forcing her chin up higher, and he deepened the kiss on her sigh.

His tongue met hers in a silky dance. A breathy moan escaped her throat, catching them both by surprise. His hand tightened on her neck, and his tongue drove into her mouth. This time it wasn't a dance. It was possession.

Ashley could do nothing but open for him and hold on to his shirt for dear life. He drew back a fraction of an inch, dragging his teeth over her lower lip on a low growl. Her knees buckled a half second before the boom of the fireworks echoed off the beach.

He steadied her, dropping his forehead to hers. She was

relieved to find his breathing as shallow as her own. Slowly, she loosened her grip on his shirt and smoothed the wrinkles. Afraid to make eye contact. What would she see? Her own desire mirrored, or something more...calculating? He was like an enemy, testing her weak spots until there was no defense left.

In her heart, she knew she couldn't hold her own. He wasn't safe. He wasn't malleable. She could lose herself to those green eyes.

This pursuit, however thrilling, could destroy her.

"Wow," she whispered and stepped back to put a little space between them.

"Yeah." He ran a hand through his hair. "Wow."

They sat down in silence.

Jason was the first to break. "That was...unexpected."

She nodded in agreement. "That's a good word for it."

"You know there's no turning back now. You can't expect to feel that and then pretend it never happened."

Ashley picked up her wine. "Please don't try to rationalize anything when my brain is mush."

"Rationalize this. I want you. I want to kiss you like that again. I want to peel your clothes off layer by layer until you are completely naked. And then I want to touch every inch of you."

"Jason—"

"I want to be inside you and feel you—"

She slapped a hand over his mouth. "For the love of God, man! Please don't finish that sentence."

He dragged her hand down. "I can't make my intentions any clearer than that."

"I'm confused. Do you want me to spy on my fiancé or get naked with you?"

"Both. I thought that was obvious."

"I just don't see how those two relationships can co-exist."

"Ashley, you can have anything you want in this life."

"I'm pretty sure I can have anything just not *everything*."

"Let's find out."

He cupped her face and leaned in again. This time soft, sweet. His mouth gently explored hers while his thumbs brushed her jawline.

She opened for him just as she knew she would. It was inevitable.

When his tongue brushed hers, she felt herself sigh.

The crackle of the fire and his touch warmed her skin.

This was what she craved. *Connection. Heat. Lust.*

The icy numbness cracked around her heart.

"Jason." She whispered his name against his mouth. "I need to think. About this."

"About us," he clarified.

She nodded. "About us."

"Don't think too long."

"How can you be so sure about this?"

"I know what I want." He shifted and drew her into his side. "And what I want is you."

"But for what? Besides sex. Unless it's just sex."

"I think sex is a fine place to start," he said, rubbing her arm through the jacket. "But it's not the only thing I have in mind."

"You're not saying a relationship, are you?" Her eyebrows skyrocketed.

"You look surprised, and not very pleased. Who would have thought just sex would be the less offensive idea?"

"I'm not offended, just...skeptical." *Confused. Terrified.*

"Let me make this as clear as possible so you don't have to overanalyze anything. I like you. I want you. And I don't share."

Share? Ashley took a moment to picture him sleeping with her on a Tuesday and then someone else—probably an incredibly tall, stacked exotic beauty with a PhD—on a Wednesday.

"Fair enough. I still need some time to think. Sex and relationships are two things I don't jump into."

"I'm feeling generous. Take a minute to think about how good it will feel when I slide my hands down—"

She covered his mouth again. "Believe me when I say I'll be thinking of little else. Now shut up."

His eyes glinted, and she felt his lips curve against her palm. He kissed her hand before taking it in his. "I really do like you."

"I kind of like you, too, Jason. Even though I'll probably live to regret it."

They stayed for a while longer, talking quietly and listening to the music. When it was time to go, Ashley palmed the cork and slid it into her bag. No matter what happened, tonight was worth remembering.

19

*A*shley stayed in bed until Steven left Monday morning as much to avoid talking to him as to cling to the sexy dreams she'd had through the night. She might be a woman scorned, but she was also a woman desired.

And that did something to keep her from being eaten alive by anger.

Vengeance also helped.

In the bathroom, she spotted Steven's new watch under a damp hand towel. She picked it up to admire the face again. Only Steven would leave a $10,000 watch carelessly shoved under a wet towel.

Her fingers skimmed across something on the back. She flipped the watch over and spotted the engraving. It was just a single initial in a stylized script. *V.*

Gross. It was time to start digging.

First things first. Ashley poured herself a giant mug of coffee and surveyed the living space from the kitchen.

Steven's "office" was set up in the corner, a disorganized mess of wires, electronics, and dirty dishes. When she had first moved in with him, she fell for the "too busy to clean up" excuse for the first month before she realized he was just a slob. A dirty, teenage boy of a slob.

She would start there in the midst of the mess. She had three hours of snooping time before she had to get ready for her closing shift today.

There was a TV and gaming console crowding a smoked glass stand. Both got significantly more use than the desktop computer tucked into the corner of the desk littered with papers and takeout containers.

She restrained herself from tossing a week-old Chinese box into the trash and sank down in the desk chair. She didn't want to make it look like she had been snooping, but she was going to have to go through everything piece by piece and put everything back in its chaotic place.

She grabbed her phone and snapped a picture of the desk from multiple angles. Satisfied that she would be able to put everything back in approximately the right place, she dug in. Takeout containers were moved to a stack on the floor. Junk mail went in another. Papers that could be interesting went into a third.

She paused every few minutes to snap a picture of the newest layer of debris.

From what she could tell there wasn't anything of investigative value besides a few alarmingly high credit card balances—thank God she wasn't marrying *that*—and a paper copy of his college fraternity newsletter upon which he had sketched Hitler mustaches and penises on the alumni pictures.

Finally reaching the top of the desk, Ashley slowly rebuilt her piles.

She wasn't even sure what, if anything, she would find. She kicked back in the chair and savored the last sip of coffee.

How dumb was he?

Extremely. Life-threateningly.

The memory of "helping him" through their bio course in college came to mind. "Babe, just let me sit next to you during the test. You know I don't do well with exams. Oh, hey, can you write up this lab for me, too?"

She snorted to no one. "Victoria has no idea what she's getting."

Ashley knew better than anyone how good Steven looked on paper versus in reality.

She shook it off. It was better to find this out now than to be a complete idiot herself and marry the asshole.

Her eyes landed on the desktop monitor. "Check his computer for emails, browsing history, anything you can think of," Jason had told her.

She jiggled the mouse and the screensaver of the new Jaguar model dissipated into a password screen.

She held her breath. He had had the same password since college and used it for everything, but wouldn't he be more careful now that he was up to something?

Password123.

Nope. Not more careful at all.

Access granted, she surveyed the desktop icons. Nothing was labeled Corporate Secrets or Insider Trading or Having an Affair.

She took the tiny flash-drive-looking device that Jason had given her and plugged it in. It was only a slight circumvent of the law. The deal was she would do a cursory scan while imaging the hard drive. Jason would run a deeper search on it and point her in the direction of any suspicious files or emails so she could "discover" them herself.

There were hundreds of messages that dated back three years. Apparently, Steven had never thought to clean out his inbox. Ashley rolled her shoulders and dug in. There were messages from his football fantasy league from two years ago, hundreds of Amazon order confirmations, and too many email chains from his fraternity brothers to count.

She decided to focus on messages from the past six months first, and if she came up empty, she would tackle older ones. Wishing she could organize as she went, Ashley settled for opening the preview pane and skimming.

After half an hour of fruitless, mind-numbing skimming, she finally stumbled across an email that stood out.

> *To: steve.noll@emax.net*
>
> *From: pbardman@corelink.com*
>
> *Great running into you Friday. It's always awesome to see a brother in our natural habitat (bar). Let me know if you want to hang out. It'll be like old times. Well, if they let junior CPAs leave the office during tax season. And as if tax season isn't bad enough, now we've got this extra work piled on for the next few months. Things were a lot easier when we were in school and had pledges to do all the work.*
>
> *Phil Barden*

Phil Barden was one of Steven's fraternity brothers. He graduated two years ahead of Steven and Ashley only knew Phil from when he returned to campus for Homecoming and Alumni Weekends.

She frowned. If Steven had run into Phil, he hadn't mentioned it to her, and that in itself was strange. She grabbed her phone and opened Facebook. The Alpha Gamma brothers of Chapter Theta were diligent about updating their Facebook page with "small world" photos of their run-ins with other alumni.

She scrolled back through the page's posts to February but didn't find a picture or a post of Steven or Phil.

Interesting.

It was possible—in fact, the odds were highly in favor—that Steven just forgot to mention the run in to her. Or that he was too drunk to remember even running into Phil. But something felt weird to her.

She clicked on Phil's Facebook profile. It was set to private so she only saw a few pictures of him at the beach and a football game. She switched back to Steven's computer and brought up LinkedIn.

Philip Barden was a junior accountant at a big accounting firm downtown where he had been for the past four years. Not much suspicious about being an accountant, Ashley mused. From what she remembered, Phil was a pretty benign guy. He didn't seem like the type to get embroiled in legal scandals.

But then again, was she really any kind of judge of character?

She leaned back in the chair, jiggling her leg. What was she missing?

Her phone signaled a new email.

Good morning, beautiful,

Attached is a copy of S's work calendar for the past few months. I highlighted all of the "meetings" he had scheduled with V in case that helps.

Jason

P.S. I'm still thinking about you. And last night.

She let herself bask in the warm glow of that last sentence for a minute. She had stayed up half the night remembering the feel of his arms around her, his mouth on hers. It felt like a dream.

Unfortunately, like all dreams, she had to wake up sometime. And when she did, it was next to a snoring dirtbag.

Ashley opened the file on her phone and scrolled through it. The highlights started in February and became more frequent before ending abruptly in April. She scrolled back again. The first "Lunch with V" was on February 16. The day after he ran into Phil.

Coincidence? What could Victoria and Phil possibly have in common?

She crinkled her nose. She was getting nowhere. She made note of the email and its date before returning to the inbox and scanning through the rest of the messages in the time frame.

Nothing else stood out.

She moved on to Steven's Facebook account. *Password123.*

His newsfeed and posts on his wall were made up of mostly college friends. No surprises there. She located Phil Barden as one of Steven's friends and reviewed their interactions. Nothing suspicious there. Photo likes, random comments. But nothing suspicious.

She opened his messages. *Jackpot.* Steven obviously never thought that anyone would poke through his stuff. There were dozens of messages to and from Victoria dating back to February.

She started skimming. And getting angrier.

If there had been any doubts about Steven's relationship with Victoria, the messages cleared those right up. It was also obvious who was in charge. Victoria set the times and places to meet, she instructed him on work issues, and she picked out his clothing.

"Wear the red tie tomorrow. I like how it looks with your navy jacket."

The messages that really got Ashley's blood boiling were the ones that mentioned her.

"It's sad that she thinks her little job could ever be as important as your career."

"How did you ever let her leave the house like that? I couldn't look at her without laughing at that ridiculous outfit. Pathetic. You know I'd never embarrass you like that in public."

And of course, Steven's compassionate response.

"When you have the deal locked down, I'm all yours. I'm looking forward to starting a new job and a new life. With you!"

He was using Ashley as a pawn in a power play with his new girlfriend. The man was a pig. They were both disgusting and deserved everything they got.

She checked the time. She had a few more minutes before she needed to get ready. She decided to take a cursory look at Steven's browser history.

She had no idea there were that many porn sites on the Internet. And her fiancé had visited every single one of them.

Scrolling through the history, she saw a Facebook address that stood out from the xxx's. Steven had visited it repeatedly and even bookmarked it.

She clicked the link and, recognizing the picture in an instant, felt her stomach drop. Georgie, her best friend, looking tan and happy on a beach in Cabo in large sunglasses and a very small bikini.

That jackass was jerking off to her best friend.

20

*A*shley parked in the garage two blocks over and attempted to use the walk to meditate her way out of the funk. It didn't work.

When she arrived at the store, she was still furious and had the beginnings of a pounding headache, which got worse when she noted two black SUVs parked out front. Both with understated Baine Security decals.

Ashley pushed her way through the door and nearly tripped over the leg of a ladder.

"Sorry about that," chirped the man—very young man, she noticed—atop the ladder. He scampered down from his perch and extended his hand. Realizing he still held a screwdriver, he stuffed it in his pocket.

"You must be Ms. Sapienza. I'm Dax. Mr. Baine told me to give you a grand tour."

"Dax?" Was that short for something? Daxter? "What does Mr. Baine want you to give me a grand tour of?"

"Your new security system." He waved his arm expansively around the store, and she noted several discreet surveillance cameras.

"Ashley! My dear!" A tall woman with a jaunty caftan and dark curly hair made a beeline for Ashley.

"Barbara! When did you get back?" She threw her arms around the woman and squeezed. "I thought you weren't coming back until next week."

"We cut our trip short so John could make his forty-fifth high school reunion this weekend. But enough about me. Isn't this wonderful?"

Ashley glanced around the store and spotted two other Baine employees tinkering with electronics and tablets.

"What is all this?"

"Your friend Mr. Baine contacted me. He said he knew the store's system needed an upgrade, which it desperately did, and that he had a new system that needed to be tested." Barbara clapped her hands together, sending a half dozen bangles jingling.

"Jason gave us a security system?" Ashley closed her eyes and took a deep breath.

"He did!" Barbara clasped her hands together. "We're paying a nominal monthly monitoring fee, which he wasn't going to charge us at all, but I insisted."

The front doorbell announced a new arrival. Barbara glanced past Ashley. "I'll help these ladies. Dax, you can give Ashley the grand tour. We'll catch up later." She winked and sailed off to greet the customers.

"Ms. Sapienza," Dax approached. "If you have a moment, I'll show you the system."

Forty minutes later, Ashley escaped down the back hallway. She was just going to take a few deep breaths and try not to murder anyone. The only ones within murdering distance were just collateral anyway.

First, peeling back the layers of Steven's deception and disgustingness, making her feel like the biggest idiot in the world. And now, Jason was sweeping in and invading her workplace. Damn it. Dwell was her sanctuary. She didn't need interference here. *What the hell was he thinking?*

She shoved the back door open, startling a sleek blonde in a fitted gray suit.

"I'm sorry! I didn't realize anyone was out here." Ashley stepped out into the alley.

The woman lifted her gaze from the tablet in her hands. "Do me a favor," she said in a clipped British accent. "Stand here and let me see if this works."

"I take it you're with Baine, too."

"Of course," she said, frowning at the screen. "Okay, now lift your face."

Ashley raised her chin. "Um, exactly what are you testing?"

"Mmm-hmm, now turn around and face the door," she said, gesturing without looking up from the screen. "Okay, look down and slowly turn around."

Ashley complied, feeling like a dancing monkey. "Stop. Keep your face down. Okay, that's good." She nodded, still frowning, and made a few more swipes across the screen. "Excellent." She tucked the tablet under her arm and extended her hand. "Patricia."

"Ashley." Her handshake was firm, no nonsense.

"Right then, Ms. Sapienza. I'm sure Dax has given you an overview of the system. So let me just show you how this particular piece of it works."

She turned the tablet toward Ashley. "Here you'll see a video feed of the back door. It's a relatively wide angle. When there is movement detected, the system automatically begins recording until the movement ceases."

Ashley nodded in feigned interest. She was still preoccupied with her roiling anger.

"Now, this is a new feature that's still in development, but Mr. Baine thought this would be the right system to test it on." Patricia selected a video on the screen and pushed play.

Ashley watched as camera footage of the back door of the store rolled. She spotted Patricia alone, huddled over the tablet just before the door burst open and she stepped out.

The camera immediately zoomed in and locked on her face.

"Wow."

"Indeed," Patricia nodded. "This is the beginning of a line of facial recognition projects that my department has been working on. The cameras lock on to the face and try to capture it from as many different angles as possible. It's going to make recognizing individuals from security footage much more efficient."

"That's impressive."

Patricia nodded briskly. "Mr. Baine seems pleased with the project."

"Right. Mr. Baine." Ashley didn't care how pleased Mr. Baine was with anything. She was going to have a loud chat with him about boundaries. "Well, thank you, Patricia. If you'll excuse me, I think I'll go talk to Mr. Baine."

21

*B*arbara had no problem letting Ashley leave to "discuss the system" with Jason. "Please tell him thank you from all of us," she reminded her on her way out the door.

"Why isn't anyone else upset by this?" Ashley muttered to herself as she pulled out of the garage. It felt like a debt. Who would give so generously without expecting something in return?

Jason's office building wasn't hard to find. It jutted into the downtown skyline in sleek, sharp lines. The heavy glass doors opened to a marble-floored lobby and a bank of elevators just beyond a security desk. She paused long enough to watch the tide of people entering and exiting with swipe cards.

Swipe-card-less, she opted for the security desk. "Excuse me, I need to go to Baine Security."

"Of course, ma'am," the desk attendant said politely. "May I see your ID please?"

She passed him her driver's license and held her breath. She wasn't going to be on any list. She should probably just text Jason, ask him to come down, and then cause a scene in the lobby.

"Ms. Sapienza, you are cleared to visit Baine Securities. Mr. Baine left you a passcard, which is yours to keep so you can come and go as you please."

"I'm sorry, I wasn't expecting to be on the list. I didn't tell Mr. Baine I was coming."

The guard chuckled. "If you're trying to surprise him, don't bother. Nothing gets past him."

So he was expecting her. For some reason that pissed her off even more. Ashley strode toward the elevators, ready for battle.

The doors opened, and she found herself face to face with him. All six feet three inches of perfection. And he absolutely did not look surprised.

Jason reached for her hand, which rose automatically to meet his even as she shook her head.

"Ashley. I'm glad to see you. Come upstairs." He pulled her back into the elevator with him while she continued to shake her head.

A crush of people joined them inside, nearly all of them nodding at or greeting Jason by name. He returned their greetings, using their names, because, of course, he *would* know everyone. He still maintained a tight grip on her hand.

"How did you know I'd be here?" she said, keeping her voice low as the elevator rose.

He shrugged and kept his gaze forward.

She let the adrenaline carry her up the eleven floors to where Baine Security occupied the building's top two floors. When the doors opened, Jason pulled her toward the front desk.

"Good afternoon, Mr. Baine," chirped the young man behind the desk of Baine Security.

"Will." Jason nodded in greeting and, without pausing, hauled Ashley down the hallway.

She had a feeling the front desk guy was dialing everyone in the office about seeing Mr. Baine drag a woman around the office. Unless this was a daily occurrence.

Jason stopped abruptly, and Ashley smacked face-first into his very solid back. He pulled her around to his side. "Ashley, this is Mona. Mona, this is Ashley. Ashley is the reason you are so happy with your birthday gift."

She smiled reflexively at the woman behind the huge desk that guarded a pair of frosted glass doors. Her silver-streaked hair was pulled back in a severe bun. Her jacket fit her slim shoulders in a precise way that hinted at custom tailoring. Her face gave nothing of her age away. Sharp blue eyes measured Ashley behind stylish glasses.

The glass vase filled with a spray of pink calla lilies dominated the front corner of her desk. Lorenzo had outdone himself, Ashley noted.

"So you're the one who deserves the credit," she rose from her chair and eyed Ashley.

Ashley had the fleeting feeling that she was a noisy student come face-to-face with the librarian.

"Thank you for the lovely gift," Mona said, her face softening into a motherly smile, and Ashley felt herself relax.

"You're so welcome. Jason knows you very well and gave me good information to make suggestions on. He obviously cares about you very much."

"I told you you'd like her." He winked at Mona and pulled Ashley toward the doors behind her.

"Wait a minute, Jason. Before you drag Ms. Sapienza into your lair, don't forget your three o'clock, and I have the forms from the lawyers for your meeting tomorrow morning. So don't leave the office without them."

Why did everyone call her "Ms. Sapienza" here? Was there a memo? Ashley also thought it was interesting that Mona was the only person in the building who called Jason, "Jason."

He frowned and glanced at his watch. "That's fine. Have the papers sent down to my car."

"It was nice to meet you, Ms. Sapienza."

Jason pulled Ashley with him through the glass doors.

"It was nice to meet you, Mona. I'm glad you like the vase—"

Her reply was cut off by the closing doors.

She whirled on Jason. "That was rude! And speaking of, what's with you invading my store with a security system that I didn't ask—"

His mouth was on hers, cutting off her tirade and train of thought. Jason cupped her face and moved his lips over hers in an urgent assault.

She melted into him, hands gripping the lapels of his jacket. His had her by the hips, pulling her tighter against him. "I've been thinking about doing this since last night," he said between kisses.

Ashley grabbed on to what was left of her common sense and pushed him back a pace.

"Why did you give us a security system?" She couldn't cover the breathlessness in her voice, but she did manage to work up a glare.

"Isn't that like asking why did you throw the life preserver overboard to the drowning sailor?"

"No. It's like asking why you installed a security system worth tens of thousands of dollars in a little retail shop without asking for anything in return."

"You're angry."

"No shit, genius. Of course I'm angry!" She spun around to pace the expansive office. "You went to my boss, behind my back. You invaded the store with your team of tech nerds. And you didn't even say a word to me about it. We're supposed to be keeping our distance from each other." She ticked the items off on her fingers. "Not to mention that isn't some run-of-the-mill home security system. I can't even imagine what it costs."

He frowned thoughtfully. "So, you're upset because I went to a business owner with a mutually beneficial proposal that would keep you and your co-workers safer while working. And then had the audacity to have my team of professionals install a very adequate security system. All without consulting the business's manager, who also happens to be the woman I want to sleep with."

Ashley sputtered. Verbal arguments were not her strong suit. She always lost herself to the mad and then spent the next several hours coming up with brilliant comebacks in the mirror.

She could feel herself losing ground. "You should have asked me."

"You would have said no."

"And why is that?"

"Because you would feel like it's too expensive of a gift and too much of an interference with your job, which is quite possibly the only place you feel in control. Also, you probably don't want to face speculation about what the 'hot security expert' is doing lurking around you and your store."

She bit her lip. Yep. That was pretty much her argument.

"So you knew I'd say no and why I'd say no, yet you did it anyway?"

"You're working in an environment that does little, if anything, to mitigate threats." His tone was clipped now.

She opened her mouth to interject, but he continued.

"Your store's system was lacking, which, in this city isn't

just careless, it's dangerous. I happen to have the resources to correct that. Everyone wins."

"It's invasive. It's...And why the hell are you so concerned over the store's safety?"

"*Your* safety," he corrected, temper beginning to show. "I want you safe." He crossed to her.

"What about people speculating about us?"

"Let them." He pulled her into his arms. "I want you. And I want you to be safe."

Ashley felt her resistance waiver. She couldn't think with him so close, his hands on her.

"What about Steven? Victoria? What if they find out you magnanimously gave me this invasive gift?"

"When is the last time Steven took any interest in what you do?"

Ouch. That hurt.

"Damn it, Jason."

They grappled in the embrace. Anger warred with lust. Ashley felt him hard against her belly and she couldn't stop herself from pressing against him. Jason's hands coursed down her back, crushing her to him. His hands slid lower still, over her behind and down to the hem of her skirt. With skill, he slid his hands under her skirt and back up, bunching the material around her waist and leaving her legs bare.

Their mouths warred, straining for more. His hands returned to her ass, squeezing. He lifted her against him and she wrapped her legs around his waist.

Her lacy thong provided no real protection.

He carried her over to a long, low sofa and collapsed on top of her. He settled between her legs, pressing his erection against the very center of her heat. The only noises were heavy, desperate breaths and the occasional whimper or growl. He yanked open her blouse with force and filled his hands with her breasts. Too much of a distraction, the soft cups of her bra were shoved down to bare her curves to him.

Ashley reached down to cup him through his pants. He groaned, and she gripped him harder.

"I want you," he growled low as his mouth settled over her nipple. There were no gentle tastes. He latched on and began to suck. She arched against him, offering him everything and wondering if it was possible to die from too much pleasure.

It had *never* been like this.

She needed to be closer. Needed to feel his skin against hers. Needed him to drive inside her and make her forget everything.

His mouth moved to her other breast while his fingers found her first nipple still damp. He tugged and rolled even as he took the other aching tip between his lips.

"Jason, please! I need you." Yep. She was definitely going to die from this. Too much want and need wrapped up in a healthy dose of "this is a horrible idea."

"Say my name again. Tell me you want me," he rumbled against her flesh.

The horrible idea thing suddenly got a lot less important.

He tugged her hand free from between them and pressed against her center, ignoring the layers of clothing in the way.

"Jason, I want you," Ashley whispered on a moan. "I want to be with you."

He released her breast long enough to recapture her mouth. His tongue thrust into her mouth in a savage imitation of sex.

He rocked against her again, and she felt her sex tighten from the friction.

And then he was sliding his hand down her body, over her crumpled skirt, to her bare thigh.

She reflexively, hypnotically opened her thighs wider.

Jason rose up on his knees and stroked his fingers down one thigh, up to the silky barrier.

Ashley bucked against his touch. She needed him closer. Inside.

Two fingers slid under the thin barrier to touch her.

"God, Ashley."

"Jason, I want—"

Twin alerts from his desktop and phone broke through the trance.

"Your three o'clock is here," said Mona through the intercom.

Panicked, Ashley shoved at him. He was already off balance, and the push had him tumbling off her and onto the floor. She jumped up, smoothing her skirt down, and stepped over him.

He sprang back up. She couldn't stop staring at the hard-on trying to fight its way out of his pants.

He attacked his tie, which was wildly askew. "Goddammit, Ashley."

"This is *my* fault?" Temper threatened to snap again as her fingers stumbled over the buttons on her blouse.

He gave up on the tie, grabbing her wrist instead. "You make me forget everything." He planted a hard kiss on her mouth and seemed ready to move in for more.

She put a hand to his mouth. "You're forgetting again. Focus, Baine."

She watched the glints of gray and brown in his eyes sharpen. Jason kissed her hand before releasing her.

She made *him* forget. With a man as in control as Jason Baine, that was a feat. She reached up and straightened his tie. "To be continued?"

"To be continued," he agreed. "Soon." It was a promise. Or maybe a threat.

Jason took his time smoothing her skirt down over her hips and straightening her blouse. "I think I lost one of your buttons." He grinned, looking not at all apologetic.

She held the gapped fabric together. "Good thing I have a sweater in the car."

She looked up and caught his smug grin. "Don't think that this gets you out of explaining exactly how installing a ridiculously expensive security system in my place of business is not an inappropriate invasion of privacy."

"I want you safe at all times." He said it matter-of-factly, and it sent her heart skipping and sliding. Romance and logic did battle. He cared. Enough to want to keep her safe. But it was the kind of over-the-top gesture that made her feel uncomfortable, indebted.

"How did you get this past Barbara?"

"Barbara isn't nearly as cynical and suspicious as you are. It was a simple transaction. She needed an upgrade to her system, and I happened to have one that was ready for testing before releasing it."

"Jason there's a fingerprint scanner."

"I didn't think you'd like the retinal scanner. Did Dax show you how to arm it from your phone?"

"I'm still not happy about this."

"I know, and I'm grateful you're willing to indulge me."

"Thank you for your very generous, very unexpected gift," she said primly.

"Are you talking about the system or what just happened on the couch?"

Ashley smacked his arm.

"Then you'll humor me when I give you these." He crossed to his desk and picked up a manila envelope.

Ashley peeked inside. "Parking passes?"

"For you and the rest of the girls at the shop. Now you can

park on the street close to the store instead of walking to the garage at night."

She sighed heavily.

"Are you getting mad again?" He tipped her chin up.

She shook her head. "I think I'm madded out. Now I'm just tired. And since we're exchanging strange gifts, here's yours." She fished the flash drive out of her bag and handed it to him.

"I haven't found anything incriminating yet, but we will. He's not very bright."

"Not if he let you go," he said, kissing her hand again.

Very smooth.

Jason wrapped an arm around her. "Come on, I'll show you the back way out of here so you don't have to meet seven Austrian businesspeople while looking like you were just mauled."

22

The next few days flew by, leaving little time for spy games or obsessing over Jason, but Ashley managed to still do a bit of both. The forensic imaging of the hard drive would take some time, so she tried to carve out an opportunity every day to comb through Steven's Facebook account or drawers or car.

She was itching to take another pass at his computer at home but hadn't found a safe opportunity to do so.

Something had to happen soon, though. After enduring a takeout night at home with him, which he tried to turn into sex, she was pretty sure she wouldn't be able to keep it together for much longer. She'd had to fake a violent migraine and lock herself in the bedroom.

One of them was going to end up dead. Him from murder or her from an aneurysm.

She hadn't seen Jason since Monday and found her thoughts wrapped up in him more often than on Steven and the present situation. She felt like a dopey teenager with a crush on the dreamy high school quarterback.

She couldn't afford to lose her focus, she told herself.

Once Steven was out of her life, *then* she could decide if she wanted to explore Jason. Every glorious inch of him.

But in order to get to potentially naked and probably spectacular Jason, she was going to have to stop avoiding Steven and start dragging information out of him.

The best way to do that was to cook a big meal and pump him full of alcohol.

Arriving home, she found Steven engrossed in a reality show. "Hey, babe," he called from the couch.

She hefted the grocery bags onto the counter. "Hey." She spotted an empty glass on the coffee table in front of him. *Perfect. He had already started.*

She wandered over to the bar and poured a generous scotch for him and grabbed a bottle of wine for dinner. "I'm making spaghetti tonight."

"Awesome," he said, attention still on the screen.

She put the drink down in front of him and took his empty glass to the kitchen where she unloaded the groceries.

Usually, when she made spaghetti, she used her grandmother's recipe for sauce. But she didn't want to taint a family tradition by making it for an undeserving dumbass, so she went for store-bought instead.

Ashley opened the wine and poured two glasses before sliding the garlic bread into the oven.

She added the pasta to the boiling water and turned the sauce down to a simmer. Cooking always relaxed her. But not tonight.

While her fiancé scratched his balls and watched horrible people on TV scream at other horrible people, she reached into the pocket in her bag to make sure the new gadget Jason messengered to her today was still secure. This little drive was for Steven's cell phone. But the only time he didn't have it on him was when he was sleeping.

She was just supposed to plug it in, let it sync, and it would somehow magically copy all of Steven's texts and browser history. Again, it was a slight—total—circumvention of the law. But she was willing to bend the truth if it meant she could get her life back, Steven-free.

God. Steven-free. Where would she live? Not in this concrete-floored, soulless façade. She wasn't leaving Dwell. But on her income, she couldn't afford to live anywhere conveniently.

The timer on the oven buzzed as she drained the pasta. She plated up the spaghetti and store-bought bread and carried it to the table.

"Dinner's ready."

She made a return trip to the kitchen for the bottle of wine.

Steven pried his ass off the couch and shuffled to the table staring at his phone.

It was time to work.

He dug in, and Ashley made sure to keep his wine topped off. "So how was work today?" She crunched into a piece of garlic bread and stuffed down the ever-present nausea she felt whenever she looked at his stupid face.

"Same old," he said, reaching for his glass. "It's a joke. I put all this time and effort in, and the partners just reap the rewards. I get nothing out of it."

"Your last bonus was pretty decent," she ventured.

"Chump change. Literally," he snorted. "It's almost embarrassing. You know what a junior partner takes home? It's like triple what my paycheck is. And *those* bonuses are something worth talking about."

"Why do you think they aren't making you partner track?" She toyed with the pasta on her plate. *Besides the fact that you're an ass and doing something illegal, of course.*

He wiped his mouth on his napkin and picked up his glass again. "Victoria says they're just trying to get everything they can out of me. Like I'm some kind of servant. They're doing the same thing to her."

She couldn't believe his nerve—or was that stupidity?—that had him so casually mentioning his mistress's name to her.

"She's family. Isn't she guaranteed to make partner?" She couldn't quite bring herself to say the evil monster's name.

"She thinks that's why they're so much harder on her. That's why she wants to leave. So she can prove to her grandfather that she's more valuable than he thinks she is."

"Do you think it's because she's not actually family?" *And just trying to take advantage of tenuous connections because she's a shitty human being.*

"They just feel threatened. But they'll be sorry when we leave."

Ashley poured more wine into his glass and figured what the hell before topping her own off.

"So Victoria's leaving the company, too?" She congratulated herself on not gagging on the shithead's name.

He nodded and reached for another piece of garlic bread. "Yeah. She's the one who got the line on some partner-track jobs."

She kept her gaze on her plate. "What firm are you looking at?"

He shrugged. "Don't know. She said she has some details to work out first." He wiped his mouth again and finished off the rest of the wine, kicking back in his chair. "Soon I'll be calling the shots. That's what I care about."

~

SHE'D THOUGHT about setting her alarm for the middle of the night but was afraid it would wake the soundly sleeping Steven next to her. Fortunately, she hadn't needed the alarm. Ashley hadn't even closed her eyes since she climbed into bed hours earlier.

Lying here in the dark sharing a bed with the man she'd been prepared to marry was killing her. She could feel the cells in her body rioting against the poison.

She needed answers and then she could start over.

She held her breath and tiptoed over to Steven's nightstand. His breathing was deep and even. The occasional snore reassured her that he was out.

Carefully, she lifted the phone from the table. She waited for another snore before unplugging the charger. She hugged the phone to her chest to block the light of the screen and quietly left the room.

In the dark, she scurried across the loft to Steven's workspace. While the drive read his phone, she decided to give his email another look. She hadn't snooped through his sent folder yet.

She eased onto his desk chair, wincing at the telltale squeak. To her anxious ears, it sounded as loud as a car crash in the silent apartment. She listened intently for a minute, straining for sounds of life coming from the bedroom.

Satisfied that Steven still slept the sound sleep of the soulless and guilty, she plugged the tiny drive into the cell phone's port and pushed the sync button. A blinking green light appeared, indicating the sync was in progress. Since Jason said it should take about fifteen minutes, she opened Steven's email on the computer to double down on the spying.

Something was still nagging her about his run-in with Phil. She was curious to see if he had replied to Phil's message.

She opened his sent folder and sorted it by recipient.

Bingo. One reply to Philip Barden two days after the original message was received.

Ashley previewed the email.

To: pbardman@corelink.com

  From: steve.noll@emax.net

  Hey man,

  Great to see you, too! We definitely need to get together more since we're both in the same city. So work is still shitty? It's funny that the legwork for billion-dollar acquisitions is done by a guy who puked on the ping-pong table at Homecoming two years ago. Can't hang with the pledges, can't make the big bucks like the partners. It sucks being this age where we do all the work and have none of the fun. Want to get together next Thursday and trade work stories? You can let me know on my other email sgnoll@gmail.com.

He had another email account. Ashley snapped a picture of the screen with her phone. She wanted to document her discovery step-by-step to make sure she could tell Jason where to look. She switched back to the desktop and opened a browser window. Sure enough, in the history she found several visits to Gmail.

One thing at a time, she cautioned herself. She reorganized his sent message folder by date and closed out of the program. Returning to the login page, she paused.

Steven had gone to great lengths to create a new email account to hide something important, so wouldn't it follow that he would use a different password?

Password123.

Login error. Damn it!

She leaned back in the chair and drummed her fingers

quietly on the desk. What would it be? How many tries would she have before the account locked?

She let her eyes scan the wreckage of his desk. Sticky notes, envelopes, and takeout menus. It could be written on any of them. She sighed and closed her eyes. "Think like an asshole," she whispered. "If I were a self-important, cheating asshole how hard would I work to hide something secret?"

She opened her eyes and stared down at the keyboard. *Hmm.* She peered under it. There on the desk was a single yellow sticky note.

DoubleD123.

Double D. Obviously an homage to Victoria's rack. Ashley mimed vomiting on the keyboard.

Theatrics aside, it was time to test her gamble.

Holding her breath, she typed it into the password field and hit enter. A full inbox opened on the screen.

Pay dirt! Dozens of messages to and from Victoria Van Camp and Phil Barden.

Ashley silently punched the air in victory. She had the moron now.

The drive on the phone beamed solid green.

It was done, but Ashley was just getting started.

23

*A*shley huddled over her latte in the corner of the café, praying that the caffeine would help her through the day. It was 6:30 in the morning—the butt crack of dawn—and she had been up the entire night combing through Steven's secret email account.

The coffee shop was a few blocks out of the way from home and work, so she rarely visited, but it suited her needs today.

She spotted him before he saw her. Even dressed for a workout, Jason moved with a casual authority. She had the pleasure of watching his face go from searching for her to finding her. He lit up when he saw her, and her stomach took an inconvenient nosedive into her feet.

It was going to be a good day.

Jason threaded his way through the collection of tiny tables.

"Thanks for meeting me. I like the shorts. They're a nice change from suits." She wiggled her eyebrows.

He glanced down at his gym shorts and long-sleeve t-shirt. "This is how I usually dress for a pre-dawn rendezvous."

He sat, and Ashley slid a black coffee across the table to him. "You don't look like the cream and sugar type."

"Very astute of you, investigator."

She grinned. "Hold your applause until the end, please." She passed him the phone drive and a manila envelope. "I've got something good."

His smile was easy, but she saw the sharpening in his eyes. "How good?"

"I know what they're after, who gave them the info, and what they plan to do with it."

"Seriously?"

"I'm kind of amazing." She leaned in and tapped the folder. "Here's the overview. One of Steven's college friends is a junior accountant at a firm downtown. He does grunt work to help one of the firm's clients structure an acquisition. A billion-dollar tech startup. The deal is top secret and going down at the end of next month. He runs into Steven, makes a casual comment about the deal without naming names, Steven mentions it to Victoria, and Victoria latches on. 'Get the details, find out who it is, I can use this as leverage for partnerships...blah blah blah.' She's working on selling the info to a guy—don't have his name—at a rival firm in return for cushy jobs for her and Steven."

"How much coffee have you had?"

"Six cups. Read."

She leaned back in her seat, cheeks flushed with excitement. "I went to the store at four this morning to print copies. Almost set off that damn alarm, too, until I remembered Dax's instructions for disarming it on my phone."

Jason stared at her for a long beat. "You're pretty cute when you're over-caffeinated."

She wrinkled her nose. "Just read and tell me how brilliant I am."

She settled in and watched him. The frown line between his eyebrows deepened. He skimmed methodically, without an outward reaction. But when he put the printouts down and looked at her, she could see the energy.

"You are incredible, Ashley." His voice was calm, but she heard the edge of victory. "We're going to get them."

She grinned back at him, basking in the moment. The end was near, and so was a new beginning.

"I kind of just want to rip your clothes off right now," he said huskily.

"You're going to have to hold that thought until next week, Romeo. I'm leaving for my parents' in a few hours. Anniversary weekend. I need to get out of my life for a few days."

"Monday then." He winked. "Do you mind if I make a few calls? I'll take you for breakfast afterward if you promise not to drink any more coffee."

"Perfect."

Jason took the folder with him and went outside to make his calls. She busied herself by checking her email on her phone. She hadn't checked it in two days, which was unheard of for her. But playing vengeance-led spy woman had eaten up a lot of her time.

She spotted one from her mother from the day before. Subject: Change of plans!

When Jason returned, she was slouched in her chair, arms crossed over her chest.

"What's the matter, beautiful? Run out of caffeine?"

She sighed. "No. Worse. My parents canceled. Dad surprised Mom with a stupid amazing cruise."

"That's terrible," he said, straight-faced. "What a bastard."

Ashley rolled her eyes. "Terrible is me spending the weekend with Steven who already has plans to spend it with his mistress."

"He's planning on you being gone the whole weekend?"

She nodded mournfully. "I was supposed to leave in two hours. I wasn't coming back until Sunday night."

Jason covered her hands with his. "How would you like to still leave in two hours?"

"Where am I going?" she asked with suspicion.

"Do you own any flannel?"

ASHLEY SHIFTED in the bucket seat of the Jeep and watched greenery sweep past her window. Jason was driving while directing what sounded like a conference call. It was his third call of the drive so far. But she didn't mind. It gave her time to think.

There was no doubt in her mind what this trip to Jason's cabin was going to lead to.

Sex. Of the mind-blowing, reality-altering variety.

Her pulse quickened, and her knee bounced restlessly.

She stole a glance at him. Dressed in worn jeans and a faded t-shirt, he looked approvably hot.

She was glad she had taken the time to shower, shave, and repack the bag originally intended for the trip to her parents'.

Good-bye comfy shorts and tank top. Hello matching underwear and bras.

She rubbed her palms against her jeans. Was she *really* ready to have his hands on her?

He hung up and tossed his phone into a cup holder near the floor.

"Sorry about that. Just trying to put things in motion so nothing stalls while we're away."

Ashley nodded. "Do you think we have enough for someone to start an investigation?"

"I think it's enough for some healthy suspicion. My grandfather has an old friend in the SEC, and he's going to start there."

"So we have the weekend off?"

"The whole weekend. Did you have anything in mind?" His wolfish expression told her exactly what he had in mind.

"How are you at gin rummy?"

His laugh warmed her belly.

THE ROAD to the cabin was more like a trail than a driveway. She enjoyed the winding path through the woods that was just entering the full bloom of spring. They drove into a sunny clearing, and Ashley could only shake her head as Jason brought the Jeep to a stop in front of the sprawling log home.

"You've *got* to be kidding me," she said, gaping through the windshield.

"Welcome to the cabin." He leaned over and released her seatbelt.

"This isn't a cabin. It's a log castle," she corrected. Surrounded by trees, the L-shaped home rose more than two and a half stories high. There were windows everywhere and a huge porch that wrapped around to the back of the house.

"Come on. We'll unpack after the tour." He squeezed her leg and slid out of the Jeep.

She joined him outside, admiring. The forest of trees reached up to the sky. Flowering bushes and unstructured evergreens ringed the house, and a wide flagstone path led to the porch.

Birds and squirrels chattered in the trees, but there wasn't a hint of traffic or human noise.

"I feel like we're in the middle of nowhere. Do you by chance own a small country here?"

Jason took her hand. "The closest neighbor is half a mile that way." He pointed to the west. "In the winter, you can see their lights from down at the lake."

He led the way onto the porch and fished keys out of his pocket. The heavy barn-style front doors quietly clicked open, and he stepped aside.

She entered and laughed when she got her first good look at the interior. "Oh, come on!"

He joined her in the foyer, grinning at her reaction. "Yeah, it's not bad."

"Not bad?" She snorted. The great room had a cathedral ceiling spanned by massive rough-cut beams. Leather couches and chairs faced a two-story stone fireplace in the living area that was overlooked by a loft. The kitchen and dining area took up most of the space to the right.

Daylight poured through three sets of French doors on the back wall.

She trailed her fingers over the countertops. "Roughing it doesn't usually involve granite and custom cabinetry."

"Trade-offs. There's granite, but no cable here."

She raised an eyebrow. "TV?"

"One big screen with an extensive Blu-Ray collection."

"Internet?"

"Wi-Fi, of course. Now you're just being ridiculous."

She laughed and crossed to a set of French doors. She stepped out onto the deck and took in the view. Lake, mountain, and the forest in bloom. From the railing, she felt as if she was staring into a painting.

The breeze toyed with her hair, and she lifted her face to the sun.

"This is beautiful, Jason."

"I'm glad you like it." His voice sounded husky. "I like having you here."

She turned to face him. She could see need and desire in his face. She felt it, too.

He stepped into her, hands settling on her hips. Her pulse quickened, and blood stirred.

"I want you, Ashley. More than I can say."

24

*A*shley ran her hands up his arms to his chest. She felt the thud of his heart under her palm and was reassured that it was beating. Jason Baine was actually human and not just some sexy robot.

"So about that gin rummy," she joked.

His smile was slow, sweet, and so tender that she felt the air evaporate from her lungs.

She brought her hands to his face and brushed her lips against his lightly, gently. She felt the tremor that ran through him. His fingers flexed into her hips.

And then he was kissing her. *Finally. Finally,* she thought.

Need stirred between them, charging the air.

Ashley wrapped her arms around his neck, burying her fingers in his hair. He shifted to press against her as his tongue swept inside her mouth. She was pinned between him and the deck railing. Between his rock-hard erection and the smooth wood.

Decadently, she rolled her hips against his until Jason spun her away from the railing without breaking contact with her mouth. She felt his fingers slip under her shirt. They skimmed across her stomach before streaking up her sides. Like flashes of lightning, his touch burned her skin.

He stilled his hands just under the silk of her bra. She heard a soft moan and realized it came from her. She wasn't the moaning type. She was usually a dignified lover. A quiet bed companion.

He skimmed his hands over her body and lifted her shirt. Drawing it up and over her head, he broke contact with her mouth and looked at her.

Ashley missed the heat of his body as soon as he was gone.

His hands returned to her hips and met at the zipper of her jeans. He attacked it with impatience and growled.

She smiled against his mouth. The cracks in his armor were showing, and his departure from the slow, patient seduction calmed her own nerves.

"Jason, I want you," she whispered.

"I'm here, baby." The voice was rough, but the hands stayed gentle. "I just want to see you." He drew her jeans down her hips sinking down with them. On his knees, he steadied her so she could step out of them. He pressed his mouth to the navy silk of her underwear, and she gasped.

So close. Already. Who needed foreplay when you could spend an hour confined in a car with Jason and his pheromones?

Rising slowly, he trailed kisses up her body, until he stood over her sighing mouth again.

"You're perfect." He whispered it. She didn't believe him for a second. But rational thought was rapidly being replaced with the need to jump him and tear his clothes off.

Instead, she let him rain kisses down her jaw to her neck. But the clothes tearing off thing was going to happen sooner rather than later.

His hands slid down her body to cup her butt. Squeezing,

he lifted her against him. She happily complied, wrapping her legs around his waist.

They were moving. She felt the sunlight disappear from her skin, and a moment later felt cold granite beneath her. She rocked back on the kitchen counter, skimming her hungry fingers down his chest to his abdomen. Lower still, she reached the waistband of his jeans.

He growled against her mouth, and she felt his stomach muscles quiver beneath her fingertips.

A shiver of power flickered through her. Her hands rushed to free him from the denim.

Ashley sighed against Jason's mouth and trailed her fingers over the cotton of his boxer briefs.

He groaned, long and low, and it was all the encouragement she needed to slip her hand beneath the waistband and grip his straining erection.

"Wait." His voice was a rasp.

But she ignored him. She stroked down his smooth, thick shaft, and when her hand returned to the tip, it was wet.

"Oh. My. God," she whispered against his lips, accidentally biting him.

He didn't seem to mind. He was too busy tugging her underwear to the side. And when he finally cupped her sex, part of her brain exploded.

"Gah." She'd given up on being coherent.

Ashley felt her bra strap slide off her shoulder, the cup slipped lower on the curve of her breast. His fingers pressed against her wet center. "Show me," he demanded.

She nearly tore a neck muscle yanking the other strap off her shoulder and shoving her bra down. Her nipples were already straining toward him, and she'd left any concerns at the door.

"Look at me," he whispered.

Ashley met his gaze and inhaled sharply as he drove two fingers inside her.

She gripped his erection tighter and began to stroke.

His fingers matched her pace, and when his mouth finally found her breast, her head fell back. She was completely at the mercy of the sensations coursing through her body. The sounds she was making now weren't even human.

His lips tugged at one nipple first and then the other. Jason's tongue worked its magic on the taut peaks, feeding.

She dragged him closer to her, angling the tip of his shaft against her wet center. Each stroke of her hand slicked him against her in a heavenly torture.

Once. Twice. She matched the strokes with the tugs of his mouth. "Jason! I can't stop."

"Don't fight it, baby."

On the next thrust of his fingers, she came, closing around him in warm waves of pleasure. She felt his cock twitch and pulse in her hand.

She didn't even have a moment to float on the carnal decadence because he was lifting her again. He cradled her butt in his hands. The tip of his shaft pressed against her slick folds, teasing her with every step. He took the stairs quickly, and she hoped he wouldn't trip and impale her. That erection felt like it could do some damage.

She squeezed him tighter with her legs. The need to be closer was overwhelming.

Jason shoved through a door, and she felt rather than saw the daylight that poured in through a wall of windows.

It warmed her skin like his touch.

He dropped them both on the bed, and she hiked her hips up against his. Apart by only millimeters of fabric, and it still wasn't close enough.

She tugged at his shirt, and he accommodated, severing

the connection with her mouth only long enough to pull the fabric over his head.

He sank down to her again, and Ashley relished the feel of his skin against hers. Fire to fire.

She ran her hands over his chest. Smooth, hot skin over carved muscle. She let her fingers trail lower over his stomach. She wanted to stop and just look, to take him in, but she was much too busy kissing him.

He moved his lips over her, whispering dark promises that made her open for him, cuddling his hardness against her heat.

He pulled back, watching her face as he pressed against her.

Ashley gasped and let her knees fall open to the sides.

"I'm not going to be able to stop once I'm inside you." He leaned over her and kissed her gently.

She shivered at the promise. "I am very comfortable with that," she told him.

His smile was pained.

His hips shifted back, away from her, and her fingers dug into the muscles of his arms, demanding he stay. "Jason, please!"

He slid against her again, and she locked her legs around his hips to keep him there.

"Greedy girl," he warned.

She squeezed him tighter between her thighs.

Jason turned his attention to her breasts. He trailed his fingers across the upper curves of her breasts, following with his mouth. His lips burned a path that edged the delicate lace. "Lift up, love."

In a hurry to do as he asked, she bounced to her elbows and smacked her forehead against his.

"You okay?" he asked, unhooking her bra with a deft flick.

"Fine. Great. Awesome."

Jason dipped his head to feed on her, and she lost the power of speech. She arched against him and rode the sensation.

This was what it felt like to be slowly consumed by hot licks of flames. It was excellent. Five-star. Highly recommended.

But her impatience was building. She didn't need this slow seduction. She needed him. Inside her. Moving in magical ways. She used her heels to work at the waistband of his jeans.

Ever obliging, he stripped off his pants and underwear. With his erection finally free, she couldn't stop the deep ache within her. He was huge, hard, and she wanted him to bury himself in her.

But when she made a move to wriggle out of underwear, he stopped her.

"Let me."

"Okay," she said on a gasp.

She flopped back and let him slide the silk down her legs. She opened wider for him. An invitation.

For one long moment, they studied each other, she on her back and he on his knees. His cock hung heavily, barely an inch from where she wanted him most.

"Is this really happening? Am I really here?" *Did she really say that out loud?*

"Yes," he whispered, lowering to her. His mouth found hers as the crest of his shaft probed intimately against her.

"Finally."

She wrapped her fingers around his cock. Desperate for the contact. He let her stroke and play. She watched as he closed his eyes and worked to keep his breath under control.

She stroked harder. His breathing grew more ragged, his

jaw clenched. *He was beautiful*, she thought. And he was hers even if it was just for the day, the weekend.

"God, Ashley." His voice was ragged. It made her feel powerful, making his control slip millimeter by millimeter.

His hand closed around hers. "Stop."

He shackled her wrists at her sides with his hands. "It's my turn." He lowered himself down between her thighs and placed a whisper-soft kiss there where the heat pooled.

Ashley's head dropped onto the pillow as he tasted her very center. Already she felt it building. She was too close to the edge.

His fingers probed as his mouth worked against her. With the first thrust of his fingers, she was lost. Marveling at how receptive her body was to just about anything he did.

"Jason! I can't—"

"You will." His voice was a rasp.

He ordered, and her body complied. She couldn't stop the first wave or the ones that crashed through her after it. She said his name on a gasp.

He ranged himself over her. "Say it again," he demanded.

"Jason."

He drove into her, filling her, never breaking eye contact. She cried out but kept her eyes locked on his. Full and aching, she took him in.

Finally.

They moved as one. Every breath, every sigh, every stroke, they climbed together toward the sun. She took him deeper and heard the growl at the back of his throat. His measured thrusts came harder and faster as the rhythm unraveled into a primal beat.

Her slick skin slapped against his.

They were twined, their bodies joined. Sweat mingled. Pleasure shared. It was right. Exactly right.

Ashley felt the crest of another orgasm rushing up. Felt herself tighten around his shaft.

Insanity. The way he made her feel was beyond anything she'd ever experienced. She felt strong and vulnerable. Invincible and powerless. Safe. Wanted.

She bucked against him and shattered. Over the roaring in her head, she heard him groan and felt the first jet of his release let loose deep inside her.

They grappled for each other in the crashing waves, coming together in the storm. She heard him whisper her name like a prayer.

ASHLEY WAS SPRAWLED on the bed over Jason's arm, facedown in beautiful oblivion. She felt like her body had just fulfilled its greatest purpose and now required extensive rest and feeding. Maybe some TV.

"Are you suffocating?" Jason rolled to her, running his free hand down her back to the curve of her butt.

"If I am, I'll die happy."

He gave her a gentle swat. "You can't die. We're not done yet."

She rolled over and swept the hair out of her face. "There can't possibly be more than that."

He dropped his mouth to her shoulder, kissing across her clavicle. His beard tickled her bare skin.

"There's always more, love."

And he proceeded to show her just how much more there was.

25

*H*ours later, Ashley woke to a reality better than dreams. She could feel Jason against her back. Her feet tucked neatly between his, the sheet covering them both. The angle of the sunlight slanting through the windows suggested that dusk was soon falling. Tilting her head, she found him watching her.

Feeling vulnerable, Ashley swiped a hand over her mouth to make sure she hadn't been drooling. "How long have you been watching me?"

"Just a few minutes." His finger traced a trail across her chest just above the sheet. "How do you feel?"

She gave herself a luxurious stretch. "Like I don't have bones anymore."

"Is that a good thing?"

She planted a kiss on his mouth. "A very good thing. This is an incredible room, by the way."

It was true. Though they had already spent several hours in it, this was her first good look around. The bed was a huge expanse of luxurious fabrics cradled by dark wood.

The gable end of the room housed a seating area against

the tall windows that overlooked forest and lake. A deep window seat with bookshelves beneath it tempted with the promise of a lazy afternoon.

"Do you happen to have a restroom in this hovel or is there a cozy outhouse in the woods?" She yawned.

He pointed toward one of the doors on the wall opposite the sitting area. "Through there."

When she slid off the bed, he caught her wrist, tugging her back for a kiss. "I'm glad you're here, Ashley."

"Me, too."

Still naked, she practically danced to the bathroom. And stopped in her tracks when her bare feet hit the warm slate floor. *Of course* his bathroom floor was heated, she thought.

The rest of the room was perfection, too. Dual vanities, topped in marble with glass tile backsplashes, flanked the door. The shower was a tiled room with multiple heads and jets that could easily hold eight adults. And then there was the tub. A sleek clawfoot centered in a large window overlooking nothing but forest. A fireplace was built into the wall at the foot of the tub with a candle-filled alcove above it.

She noted that none of the candles had been lit. She wondered if Jason ever used the tub. Did he ever see the spectacular view anymore? Was it something someone could ever grow used to?

When she returned to the bedroom, she stood in the doorway and leaned against the frame.

"There's only one thing that is going to make me leave this bathroom nirvana."

Jason tugged the sheet down and gave her a wicked grin.

"Okay, two things."

"Name it."

"Food."

"It looks like we were too busy for lunch today," he said, checking the sun through the windows. "Steaks for dinner?"

Ashley dashed from doorway to bed and hopped on top of him. "You had me at steak."

❧

OF COURSE there was an outdoor kitchen attached to the deck, what "cabin" wouldn't have one? Ashley shook her head while she constructed a salad. Jason seasoned steaks on the counter next to the grill.

Hunger had her snatching carrots and cucumbers to tide her over. She ran the knife through a handful of radishes and relaxed in the moment.

Jason hadn't wanted them to get dressed since they would just be taking their clothes off again, and she couldn't argue with that practicality. So they decided on robes. He had magically produced a plush white robe in her size from the massive walk-in closet next to the bathroom.

She wondered how many other women had wrapped themselves in that particular robe, but only for the briefest of seconds before dismissing the thought. She was here now, wasn't she? That's what mattered. She couldn't do a damn thing about the past or the future. But today was to be savored. Like this carrot. She crunched enthusiastically.

He glanced up from the grill. "Steaks will be done in ten."

"Salad's just waiting for dressing. I can go in and throw the potatoes in the microwave so they get done around the same time as the steaks."

"Perfect."

Yes, he certainly was. Even—or maybe especially—barefoot and robed, he still drew the eye. Now that she knew what was under the robe, she wanted him even more. Ashley pressed a kiss to his cheek as she passed him on her way to the kitchen.

He grabbed the belt of her robe, and she let him pull her closer. "I think we can do better than that," he teased.

She wrapped her arms around his neck and rose on her tiptoes to press a soft kiss to his mouth. He lifted her off the ground and deepened the kiss before setting her down gently.

"That's better."

She smiled as she walked toward the door. A man who wanted to kiss her before she left the room. What would that life look like?

She had expected and experienced the relief of release, several times thank you very much. But there was a growing awareness that none of this could last that made her want to hang on to every kiss, every moment that they had.

In the kitchen, she loaded two potatoes into the microwave. While they cooked, she decided to check her phone. She had texted Steven hours ago with the lie that she had arrived at her parents' house.

She thought it best that she let him think there hadn't been a change of plans. How ironic that both she and her fiancé were spending their weekend with their lovers.

Lover. What was Georgie going to say to that? Ashley laughed out loud at the thought of her friend's response. She would call her on Monday.

There was a text from Steven.

Steven: Cool. Tell them I said hi.

And a text from Barbara at the store instructing Ashley not to check her phone for the remainder of the weekend.

Barbara: Everything is under control. You deserve a nice, quiet weekend!

She wasn't sure if nice or quiet was the proper description for the toe-curling, angels-singing orgasms she'd had so far. But Barbara didn't need to hear those kinds of details.

Ashley: Thanks, Barbara! You're the best!

With things under control at the store, her parents out of the country, and Steven not expecting her back until Sunday night, she could afford to disconnect for a weekend.

The microwave timer beeped. She put the steaming potatoes on a plate and returned to the deck where Jason was just pulling the steaks off of the grill.

"That smells amazing," Ashley groaned, sniffing the air.

"You'd better hurry. I could eat both of these after that workout," he warned.

"I will fight you for them. Don't get between my empty stomach and a plate of medium rare Delmonicos," she threatened.

They spent the rest of the evening eating, talking, and lounging. Jason put in a movie, and they missed the ending.

Ashley was beginning to wonder if proximity meant that they would always end up naked and sated.

Still straddling him, she pressed her lips to his neck. "I don't know why I can't keep my hands off of you."

"Let's hope that never changes." He stroked his hand down her bare back.

She cuddled closer. "Ending up naked all the time really restricts the public activities we could do together."

"Mmm." He streaked his fingers up her spine, drawing

goose bumps to the surface. "No grocery shopping. No movies. No restaurants."

Ashley laughed. "The people in the café would be scandalized."

"We could never have children. The parent-teacher meetings would get us arrested," he mused.

"I guess we're just going to have to learn to control ourselves," she sighed.

"Let's not rush it." He tickled her ribs. "Maybe we can just become sex-obsessed hermits and never leave the house."

"My orgasm count says we're halfway there already," she teased.

He pinched her. "You're keeping track?"

"I like taking inventory, so I know exactly what I have."

"Well, let's see what we can do to get your numbers up." He tossed her down on the couch cushion next to him and rolled to cover her. And she stopped worrying about what would happen next or what she'd do when she couldn't have him anymore.

ASHLEY SNUGGLED DEEPER into the fleecy robe and wrapped her fingers around the cheery red coffee mug. She inhaled the scents of steamy caffeine and spring sunshine while enjoying the view from the deck. Jason was showering upstairs, and she had the view all to herself.

She felt relaxed, loose. At ease. Which was no slight feat, considering the insanity of her life. It was in shambles, but right this second it all felt worth it.

If only she didn't have to go back.

But of course she would. She would clean up the shards of the life that had been hers and move on. She didn't dare think of what the future would look like if Jason were in it. That was something she just wasn't ready to consider.

Quiet weekends at the cabin. Long nights wrapped around each other, tasting, taking. Waking up to that perfect face every morning.

She shook the thoughts from her head. *Stop considering the un-considerable*, she ordered. Underneath the perfection, Jason Baine was a man. A human one. And she knew so little about him. Could she ever settle again for a man who kept so much of his life from her? Would he even want her when he was done with Steven and Victoria?

"Good morning, beautiful."

Ashley tilted her head back against the wood of the chair and smiled lazily. "Morning, Romeo."

Fresh from the shower, Jason leaned in for a soft kiss before helping himself to some of her coffee. His sweatpants sat low on his hips, drawstring untied, and his t-shirt looked like it had endured about a decade of wear.

He looked relaxed. Something Ashley hadn't seen before.

"Two questions. How often do you work out, and how is it that my favorite creamer ended up in your refrigerator here?" she asked playfully.

"A couple of times a week and lucky guess?" He handed her the mug and leaned back against the railing.

"You would never leave anything up to luck. Do you have some kind of dossier on me?"

"A dossier?" He grinned.

"You know, a big, fat secret file with a list of my likes and dislikes." She stood, setting the coffee on the railing. She moved to stand between his legs and leaned into him. "Stuff like 'loves hazelnut coffee creamer, dislikes lima beans and zombie movies.'"

"Likes riding me into oblivion?" Jason supplied, combing his fingers through her hair.

"That's like saying 'likes sunshine and puppies.' Everyone would like that. And anyone who says they don't shouldn't be trusted."

His smile warmed her like the sun. "In that case, I love sunshine and puppies."

"That's very wise of you."

"Are you hungry?"

"Starving," she admitted. "What time is it?"

"It's 10:30. Do you want breakfast or lunch?"

"I'm hungry enough for both at this point," she said, wrapping her arms around his neck.

"Let's go see what we can find in the kitchen before I ravage you again."

"We've got to keep up our strength," she agreed solemnly.

They decided on sandwiches with bacon in a nod to breakfast and a tasty-looking pasta salad that Jason produced from the fridge.

"You certainly stocked up for this trip quickly," she teased.

"A motivated man always finds a way to get things done."

"And what was your motivation?"

"Seeing you in nothing but that robe for 48 hours was quite the motivator."

"Why Mr. Baine, flattery." Ashley fluttered her eyelashes before turning her attention back to the cold cuts.

He laughed and heaped the pasta salad onto two plates. He looked almost human here. If humans had faces—not to mention bodies—that would make sculptors weep with joy at their perfection.

Ashley ran a knife through the thick, crusty bread, and together they constructed their sandwiches.

"Is this the only place you get to relax?" She handed him a plate, and they walked through the doors to the deck.

"Sometimes. It's usually more of a time issue than location."

"I guess running the world is time-consuming." She eased down into a cushioned chair at the long wooden farm table.

"I've never had much of a reason to focus on anything but work."

Jason sat across from her, back to the view.

"You know you're missing quite an impressive view," she said, stabbing at the pasta salad with a fork.

"You're only saying that because you don't know how impressive the view is from here."

The blush tinged her cheeks as he watched her wolfishly. "That's a lame line, and you know it."

He grinned, slowly, dangerously. "I'm out of practice. Bear with me."

"You know, you've already gotten me into bed...several times. You have me here for the rest of the weekend. You don't have to go full throttle with this seduction thing."

He leaned across the table and brushed his thumb against her lower lip. "I'm just getting started."

26

They decided to put on clothes and actually leave the house for a few hours so Jason could show her the lake. Ashley was glad she had gone with her instincts and packed sneakers and shorts. She also had a little black dress, bug spray, and a stain remover pen should the need for any of those items arise.

She prided herself on being an organized planner. Things didn't usually surprise her because she explored all angles and developed contingencies before moving forward.

However, the fact that she was spending a sunny spring afternoon hiking with Jason Baine, tech and security kajillionaire, was a bit of a surprise.

An hour into a hike on a narrow pine-needle-strewn trail that meandered around the lake and she was convinced that she needed to quit her job and move out here to do whatever it was people did for a living here. Sell firewood. Launder money. Whatever. Everything was green, even the light that filtered down through the canopy of leaves.

She threw a glance over her shoulder at Jason who walked

quietly behind her, carrying a backpack with snacks and water.

"It's so peaceful here. Where are we going?"

"You'll see." He winked. "Take the next right at the Y."

She followed his directions. Of course there was a plan, a destination. Jason wouldn't do anything without an end goal in mind.

Another couple of steps and the trees thinned then disappeared altogether.

The view stole her breath. She came to a halt on a large stone outcropping that overlooked the expanse of sparkling lake water below.

Jason rested his hands on her shoulders. "What do you think?

"I think that there's no way this could possibly be real life."

He rested his chin on top of her head and wrapped an arm around her shoulders. "Then we'd better enjoy it while we can." He dropped a kiss on her hair. "Come on, let's open the provisions."

They sat on the rock and stretched out. Ashley laughed when he unpacked the "provisions."

"Chips and a package of chocolate chip cookies?"

"It's the hiking snack of champions," he insisted.

"Champion teenagers maybe," she teased, helping herself to a handful of salty chips and a bottle of water. "Where's your gourmet granola. Your premium truffle protein bars?"

"Every man has his vices."

"I would expect a man like you to have...*different* vices."

He handed her a cookie and took two for himself. "You're talking about my dickey collection again, aren't you?"

She nodded solemnly. "Yes, yes I am. You realize that as soon as I find it, this torrid affair will be over."

"I'll burn them for you. Even the monogrammed ones." He pivoted and laid his head in her lap.

She toyed with his hair, staring off across the lake. "Have you thought about what you're going to do when this is all over?"

"When what is over?"

"What's it going to do to your family when you have your stepsister arrested?"

"It's going to make Thanksgiving dinner a lot more tolerable."

Ashley tugged his hair. "I'm serious. What do your grandfather and father think about what's happening?"

He sighed. "My grandfather worked very hard to make a place for Victoria, who never deserved one, in the family and his company. I think he was trying to make up for my father's carelessness.

"He married Victoria's mother, Sylvia—presumably for her ex-husband's money—and immediately began cheating on her. They were together for barely two years when he cheated on her with some widowed socialite with a drug problem who told everyone about it. The divorce was messy. My grandfather put Victoria through college to make up for it. And then she guilt-tripped him into a job at the firm."

"Who's the bad guy in that story? Your father or Victoria?"

"Neither of them is an innocent victim." He was staring off into space, a hard expression on his face. Ashley ran a finger over the line between his eyebrows to smooth it away.

His gaze returned to her, and his face softened. "What are you going to do when Steven is out of the picture?" He tugged on a strand of her hair.

She squinted out over the vista, wondering if just the thought of the man who'd lied and cheated could taint the air. "I honestly don't know. I ended up here because of Steven's job, so without that restriction, I could go anywhere. But I love the store. I love what I do there. And the city feels like home. I don't really see myself packing up and leaving town."

"I was hoping you'd say that." Jason took her palm and brought it to his mouth. "I'm also hoping you'll be interested in seeing what we're like without them."

"Hmm. You mean, keep all this?" She gestured at the view, ignoring the way her heart started to pound. "I don't know. It would be such a hardship."

He reached up to tickle her ribs. "Smartass."

She laughed and wrestled his hands away.

"Tell me you'll still be here after this is over."

"It's going to depend on how emotionally scarred I am," she teased. Humor was her last defense.

He moved so quickly, she didn't have time to defend herself. Ashley found herself flat on her back with Jason straddling her. He pinned her arms over her head easily with one hand. His other hand roamed her side. "Tell me or I tickle."

She squirmed under him. "I'll scream!"

"And what? Hundreds of small woodland creatures will leap to your defense in song?" He grinned and began his assault. She did scream, but to no avail.

"Okay, okay, okay! I'll be here!"

"Promise me." He dug a finger into her belly.

"Promise! Geez, you weirdo."

"There, that wasn't so hard, was it?" he leaned down and kissed her. It was intended to be light, playful. But the second her tongue met his, the urgency exploded.

His hands streaked over her belly and under her shirt. In his haste to touch her, he yanked hard on her bra, rending it in two.

She gasped against his mouth as his hand found her breast.

The growl that came from his throat was primal. She fought against the restraint at her hands, but he merely tightened his hold. "I want you here, like this."

She could feel him hard against her.

"Someone could see—"

He squeezed once, and then his fingers sought her straining nipple.

"There's no one to see. This is my land."

He tugged her shirt up. She felt the warmth of the sunshine on her breasts. And then his mouth was on her. Tugging and tasting. She bucked against him.

His free hand moved to her shorts, unbuttoning them in a swift move. She bridged up so he could pull them off. He freed himself from his own shorts before settling between her legs.

"Promise me you'll stay, Ashley," he whispered, darkly as he probed her center.

"I promise!" As soon as she gave him the words, which she wasn't even sure were the truth, he drove into her. She gasped at the invasion and bent her knees to take more.

His thrusts were swift and hard, on the borderline of losing control. The rocky ground bit into her back, but she didn't care. He filled her completely, and that was what she craved.

He suddenly released her hands and lifted her from the rock. "I don't want to hurt you." He sat up and lifted her to straddle him. "Ride." He positioned himself under her so all she had to do was sink down on him. Inch by glorious inch until he was completely sheathed in her.

He recaptured her breast with his mouth, and she rode until they came together in a swift explosion of need. It was her name that he half-shouted to the trees.

Always her name.

"I THINK I'll take a long, hot bath in that incredible tub of yours," Ashley decided when they returned to the house. "I've got pine needles and dirt in places they don't belong."

"This is the first time that tub will have been used." He put the backpack down on the kitchen island.

"You're not the 'soak all your troubles away' kind of guy?" she teased.

He laughed and guided her up the stairs, hands on her hips. "I'm more of a 'shower and solve the troubles' kind of guy."

"No one has ever used the tub? How does anyone resist that temptation?"

"I've never brought anyone besides family here."

She believed him. For God knows what reason, she was the only woman he had ever brought here. She bit her lip to keep the smile from splitting her face. So this is what it felt like to be special. To be treasured.

Jason smacked her on the butt playfully. "Come on, let's get your bath ready."

He led her into the bathroom and turned on the tub's faucet. "Keep an eye on the temperature." He handed her the robe. "Okay, beautiful. Take it all off. I'll do some laundry while you relax."

Ashley complied, tugging her shirt over her head. She had no idea where her shredded bra had gotten to. It was probably back on the trail somewhere. She shed her shorts, too, and stood naked in front of him.

His gaze warmed her skin.

He stepped forward to cup her breast, hefting it in his palm. "You are too perfect."

"Uh, you're the one drawing me a bath and doing laundry. That's textbook perfect," she argued.

He dropped a kiss on her forehead and slid his thumb over her nipple. It went taut. "God, the way you respond to me."

He stepped back abruptly. "You'd better get in the tub now before I make love to you again. Soon you'll be too sore to walk."

Ashley grinned as he gathered up her clothes and hurried out of the room. She loved that her body had this effect on him. It felt...powerful.

Pulling her hair up in a knot, she returned to the tub and slid beneath the water's surface. The steamy heat enveloped her and teased a sigh out of her.

Sunlight filtered through the tall windows, warming her face and arms. She cracked an eyelid long enough to appreciate the greens and blues beyond the window.

Perfection.

Minutes later, the snap of a camera brought her back. She spotted Jason standing inside the doorway, a tray at his feet and cell phone in hand.

"Hey!"

"Sorry to disturb you, but I had to commemorate the tub's maiden voyage. You looked peaceful." He tucked the phone away in a pocket and picked up the tray.

"I thought your bath could use some wine." He settled the tray across the tub lip.

"Now this is service," she teased, eyeing the wine and small plate of cookies.

"It's just an excuse to see you naked again."

"Insatiable."

"I could say the same about you." His hand dipped into the water to tease the pink tip of her breast.

174

Her head dropped back against the tub, and she fought a moan. "I can't help it. Every time you touch me, I want more."

"Close your eyes."

Skeptical, she raised an eyebrow but did as she was told.

"Just relax. Let me touch you."

His hand stroked over her breasts, gently tugging and kneading, before slipping lower beneath the water between her thighs.

She opened for him, knees falling to the sides. He stroked gently at first, circling her sensitive center with the pads of his fingers.

Ashley let her head loll back. Eyes closed, she drifted on the sensations.

She felt his other hand enter the water to cup her breast and sighed. It was pleasure that she floated on. Pleasure given by his gentle hands.

She felt the subtle tensing between her legs and knew he was going to take her over the edge.

"You're such a gift to me, Ashley. Let me give you this."

This time she didn't stifle her moan. She lifted her hips to press against his hand. "That's right, beautiful," he whispered. She felt his fingers probing and she opened, accepting them. They slid inside her as he tugged harder on her nipple.

"Oh, Jason," she sighed.

"Let it happen, Ashley. Let me take you." His fingers withdrew and then thrust into her again. He drove her higher until she closed on his fingers and came in slow, sweet waves. Her hands fisting in the water.

THEY SPENT the evening relaxing outside. Dinner was hot dogs and s'mores cooked over the fire in the outdoor fireplace.

Ashley licked melted chocolate from her thumb. "Who knew roughing it could be so delicious?"

Jason leaned over to pop her index finger in his mouth. "I agree."

"Hey! Get your own chocolate-smeared fingers!" She slapped at him.

They settled back and watched the fire. She took a sip of her beer. "You know, it strikes me as strange that we can be this intimate and yet I hardly know you."

"I'm pretty sure you now know every inch of my body."

Every perfect, chiseled inch. "Isn't there more to you than just a hot body?"

"Isn't that enough?" he teased.

She rolled her eyes. "Okay, Mr. Deflection. How hard do you have to work at this whole mysterious thing? Are there times when you really want to open up and tell someone about your day? Or are you just naturally a vault?"

He took a long pull from his beer. "No one is naturally a vault. It's just not easy for me to open up."

"Were you born that way, or did some girl break your heart?" she asked.

"Maybe a little bit of that. Do you trust me?"

"What does trust have to do with talking about yourself?"

"Now who's deflecting?" Jason smirked.

"Smartass."

"I think there are layers of trust. There's the casual trust where you tell someone about your day and you trust them to care enough to listen. Then there are deeper layers where some people think they can trust someone not to hurt them."

"And you think that's bullshit?"

"Don't you?"

Ashley took another swallow, frowned. "Do you think all people are untrustworthy?"

"Yes. It's just to what degree? Everyone becomes untrustworthy at some point. Whether they lie or cheat or steal or backstab. It's just better not to let yourself be vulnerable like that."

"Well, aren't you just a little ray of sunshine?"

"I prefer to think of myself as a realist. I'm surprised that you, of all people, don't agree," he said.

"I don't think that all people are going to turn out to be like Steven. At least, God, I hope they aren't. That would be an incredibly narcissistic world."

"You haven't answered my question yet. Do you trust me?"

"I don't know you well enough yet to decide."

"Touché."

27

*A*shley woke Sunday morning to a fully-dressed Jason delivering a cup of coffee.

"It's early," she groaned. "Why are you wearing clothes?"

He sat on the edge of the bed. "I have some bad news. I'm hoping the coffee will help make up for it."

"We have to go home, don't we?"

"My grandfather set a meeting with the investigators today."

"So it's almost over?"

He set the coffee on the nightstand and stroked a hand through her hair. "Almost."

She sat up and reached for the mug. "Okay. I can be ready to go in twenty."

"I'll make it up to you, Ashley. I promise."

The ride home was quiet, with both of them lost in their own thoughts. His phone rang several times, but he let it go to voice mail. He seemed pensive, perhaps almost nervous behind the wheel. The funny, relaxed Jason from yesterday was gone, closed behind his walls.

She saw a text from Georgie, from the day before asking her how her trip to her parents' was.

Ashley: Trip to parents canceled. Spent weekend in the woods for an orgasm marathon with my bearded lov-ah. Call you later!

Georgie replied seconds later.

Georgie: Squeal!!

Ashley grinned. It would be fun filling Georgie in on the details of the weekend. It made her think of her conversation with Jason about trust.

She shared things with Georgie because she knew her friend cared about her. But sometimes that same reason caused her to keep things from people. She hadn't shared any of her earlier relationship troubles with Steven with anyone. And maybe that was partly because she didn't want her friends or her parents worrying about her and partly because she didn't want them judging her for staying...or now, leaving.

She thought about how her parents would react when she told them about why she and Steven were no longer together.

Maybe sometimes withholding was kinder when it was for protection.

IT WAS JUST after nine in the morning when they pulled into Jason's driveway. One of the garage doors raised soundlessly, and he pulled the Jeep inside.

"We're back," he announced.

"Back to reality," Ashley echoed flatly.

He turned to her in his seat. "Ashley, no matter what

happens this week, I want you to remember this weekend."

"Believe me, Jason, it's burned into my brain. I'll probably still be fantasizing about this weekend when I'm 90."

He squeezed her thigh. "Good girl. I'm counting on that. Are you going home?"

"I guess so," she sighed. "I should catch up on a few mountains of laundry and dishes that I let slide while I was playing spy games. At least I'll have the place to myself until he comes home tonight."

"Are you going to stay there when this is all over?"

"I hadn't really thought about it yet, but probably not. I can't afford the place on my own and I certainly don't have any sentimental attachment to it."

He nodded. "Text me when you get home, okay?"

"As long as you text me after your meeting."

"Deal." He leaned forward. "Now give me a kiss that I'll remember."

ASHLEY ARRIVED home a little disheveled but still smiling. The kiss had gone a bit farther than she had planned. She felt like a teenager sneaking home after curfew.

A teenager sneaking home to find a pair of stilettos in a jumble with a man's belt and tie just inside the door.

She quietly set her bag down. A quick survey of the kitchen revealed two wine glasses—the good crystal ones that Steven had insisted on—and a woman's Coach clutch tossed carelessly on the breakfast bar.

Victoria.

Her heart pounded as adrenaline coursed through her system. It would end today. All she had to do was walk into that bedroom.

Taking slow, measured breaths, she sat down on a barstool. Her hands were shaking with the urge to run in there and tear the door off the hinges. But she needed to do this right. She got one chance at the perfect reaction and didn't want to think of all the things she should have done differently later.

She picked up one of the nude heels by the door and dropped it into the trashcan before grabbing a bottle of ketchup from the refrigerator.

She opened Victoria's clutch and squeezed the contents of the bottle into it. Closing the metal clasp, she set it neatly back in its place.

The walk to the bedroom door seemed to last forever. Her heart thudded in her ears as she reached for the handle.

Don't back down. Don't back down. You can do this. Oh, God. She hoped she wouldn't throw up. She took a deep breath and shoved the door open hard enough that it bounced off the wall. Two heads popped up from the rumpled bed.

"Get. Out."

Her voice must have carried a pretty high threat level because Steven and Victoria both bolted naked from the bed.

Ashley stepped into the room and grabbed the slinky cocktail dress that was in a heap on the floor. She hurled it at the retreating blonde head.

"Get out of my house!"

"Whoa, Ash! Calm down!"

Steven was busy trying to yank on a pair of pants backwards.

She advanced on him fully prepared to claw his eyes out if the need arose. "Calm down? I come home and find you in my bed with some skank from your office, and you want me to calm down?"

"Are you going to let her talk to me that way?" Victoria

shrieked, storming back into the bedroom, her dress partially on.

"What part of 'get out' don't you understand?" Ashley yelled. She grabbed the framed engagement picture off of the dresser and hurled it at the wall behind Victoria.

"Steven!" Victoria screamed.

Steven, still fighting with his pants, tripped and fell in the doorway. Victoria stormed past him with Ashley hot on her heels.

"Babe, I can explain!" He stumbled to his feet, following them down the hallway.

Ashley found Victoria frantically gathering her things in the kitchen.

"If you aren't out of here in ten seconds, I'm calling the cops."

"You have no grounds. I'm visiting my *boyfriend* in his *home*."

"Why don't you take *your* boyfriend to *your* home and get out of mine?"

"Listen, Ash, let's talk this out." Barefoot, with suit pants on backwards, Steven was pulling a t-shirt over his head.

She hurled one of the wine glasses at him.

"She's a crazy bitch," Victoria shrieked and ran for the door.

"What are you waiting for?" Ashley threw his car keys at him and hit him squarely in the forehead. "Get the hell out."

THE SUDDEN QUIET in the loft was overwhelming. Hands on hips, Ashley surveyed the mess. It was no longer hers to clean up. Thankfully, because every surface probably needed to be disinfected.

Her phone signaled a text, but she ignored it. She had things to do.

It took her the better part of three hours to meticulously pack everything that was hers. Everything that she was keeping. She called a moving and storage company for same-day pickup and gave them Steven's credit card when they named the hefty fee.

She didn't know where she was going to go. But she was done here.

She briefly thought about using Steven's credit card to put herself up in Georgie's hotel but dismissed the idea. She didn't want any more ties to him. Besides, he wouldn't be able to afford it much longer.

She took a final tour of the apartment, making sure she wasn't leaving anything important behind. It was amazing to realize how much wasn't important. She had left nearly everything, taking only what was officially hers, which amounted to three suitcases, a dozen cardboard boxes, and a few odd pieces of furniture.

While the movers loaded everything up, she calmly put her engagement ring in a sandwich bag and dropped it in her purse. It would be her down payment on a new apartment.

"We good to go here?" a gentleman named Gus asked, loading up the last of the boxes on a dolly.

"Yep. Good to go." Ashley allowed herself a small sigh as she watched her life roll out the door.

But there was no time for regrets. Or feeling sorry for herself. There was only time for forward progress.

She wrestled her bags into the elevator and hit the garage button. She had no idea where she was going to go. Maybe a hotel close to work for a few days? She would start looking for a new place in the morning. *Crap, what if she had to get a roommate?*

The elevator doors whirred open on a neon-spandex-clad Mrs. Menifield.

"Ashley, my dear! How are..." Her voice trailed off when she noticed the suitcases. "Oh, dear. I don't suppose you're going on a trip?"

"No, unfortunately, Mrs. Menifield. I'm moving out." Ashley maneuvered the first suitcase out into the garage and held the doors open for her neighbor.

"Oh, I had hoped it would be your other half moving out when you broke up," Mrs. Menifield sighed.

Ashley reached for the second bag. "I take it you're not surprised?"

Mrs. Menifield shook her brassy red head. "When you've lived as long as I have, you get good at identifying assholes. And that fiancé of yours is a big one."

"Ex-fiancé now," Ashley said, tugging the next suitcase through the doors. "And I wish I would have had your radar."

"You're a smart girl. You won't let it happen again." She wrapped a freckled hand around the handle of the last bag. "I wish you didn't have to go. Where are you moving?"

Ashley took the suitcase from her. "I'm not sure. I think I'm going to find a hotel for a few days before I start looking for a place to live."

"Why don't you stay with me?" Her neighbor's eyes lit up behind her tinted bifocals. "I've got a spare bedroom. We'd be just like Laverne and Shirley!"

"Thank you, Mrs. Menifield, but I couldn't impose—"

"Nonsense! It's perfect, and it will annoy that asshole if you stay in the building. I won't take no for an answer." She wrestled the suitcase away from Ashley and pulled it back into the elevator with surprising strength. "Now come on, we'll start happy hour early!"

28

*A*nd a happy hour it was. With her suitcases safely stowed in Mrs. Menifield's spare room, Ashley learned that every Sunday afternoon her elderly neighbor hosted a well-attended happy hour.

"How did I not know about this?" she asked the couple who lived in 3E while taking a healthy sip of her third "house special."

Michael and Mitchell ran an architecture firm and were in the process of adopting twins from Vietnam.

"It's probably because no one in the building likes your ex-fiancé," Michael said, patting her hand.

"He's kind of a douche," Mitchell agreed over the rim of his glass. "He never held the elevator for us."

"And remember when he first moved in, he parked in 2B's space for two weeks because it was 'closer to the door,' until he got a cease and desist letter from the HOA?"

Ashley smacked herself in the forehead a little harder than necessary. "I mean seriously, how is it that *everyone* was aware of that except me?"

"Honey, everyone has to learn it the hard way." Michael sighed, tilting his glass at her. "It takes balls to stay in the same building. It's going to send the girlfriend into a hissy fit."

She nodded morosely.

"What are you going to do now?" Mitchell asked.

"That's the thing," she sighed. "I have no idea! I've *always* known what was next. And now, my whole life comes to a screeching halt, and I don't know where to go from here."

"Maybe that's just what you need, then. Something unplanned. Something that'll sweep you away."

Something like Jason Baine?

Oh crap.

The Jason Baine she was supposed to text hours ago to let him know she was home safe. Where the hell was her phone anyway?

Ashley excused herself quickly and weaved her way through half the building's tenants to get to the spare room. Not finding her phone on the first dig, she upended her purse on the bed. She dove for it as it tumbled out in a tangle of loose change and now crumpled receipts.

Shit. Thirteen texts and six missed calls.

She sat down on the bed to work her way through them. She ignored the handful from Steven reminding her that *his* name was on the loft, not hers, and that technically, she couldn't kick him out of his own home. He would figure out sooner or later that it was safe to go home. And then hopefully be arrested.

She was reading through Jason's texts when the phone rang in her hand. Startled she dropped it on the floor and had to fish it out from under the bed before answering.

"'Lo?"

"Ashley? Are you all right? Where are you?"

She smiled at the worry in his voice. He really did care about her.

"I'm fine. Totally fine."

"Where are you? Have you been drinking?"

"Yes, a lot. Do I sound *in-ee-bree-ated*?" She congratulated herself on her perfect enunciation.

"You sound drunk and muffled." He sounded angry.

"Oh, that's because I'm partially under a bed. Hang on." She wiggled out and up into a seated position. "Is that better?"

"Where are you?"

"I'm at the loft, silly."

"Jesus, Ashley, my team saw Steven and Victoria leaving the building this morning. I thought they kidnapped you or killed you!"

She giggled. "That's hilarious, Jason. No kidnapping here. I got home, and they were all naked in my bed, so I threw a bunch of things at them and put ketchup in her purse and made them leave. You know I'm homeless now? I was going to stay in a hotel, but Mrs. Menifield invited me to happy hour, and now I have a place to stay!"

He was silent for a few seconds. "Mrs. Menifield. Does she live in your building?"

Ashley nodded.

"Ashley."

"Huh?"

"Does Mrs. Menifield live in your building?"

"Yes." She nodded again.

"And you moved out of your place and are staying with her?"

"Yes." Ashley nodded. "She has a spare room. It's decorated with kitties." She plucked at a pink kitten pillow.

"What about all your stuff?"

"Oh, that." She waved dismissively. "The movers took it to storage today."

"I see."

"I'm sorry you were worried. Everything is fine."

"And you and Steven are done?"

"Yep. Oh," she exclaimed a little too loudly, "speaking of Steven, how was your meeting with the investigators? Are they going to investigate?"

She heard the quiet sigh. "They want to meet with you."

"Me?" Nerves fluttered in her belly.

"They just want to talk to you about what you know about Steven's activities."

"Do they know about us? How does that make all this look?"

"They haven't asked those questions yet. And I don't think the truth is going to change whether or not they choose to investigate."

"Do I have to talk to them?" *Was this ever really going to be over?*

"I don't see a way around it, Ashley. I'm sorry."

She sighed. "When?"

"Tomorrow if possible."

"Okay. I work until 3:00."

"I'll schedule it for 3:30 at my office."

She was quiet.

"Has Steven tried to contact you?"

"A couple of times, mainly just to tell me I don't have any right to throw him out of his house. I imagine he's back now, unless he decided to stay with Victoria."

"Tell me if he doesn't leave you alone. Okay?"

"I will. So what are you doing tonight?"

"You mean now that I don't have to track down your kidnappers? I'm going to go talk to my grandfather and his lawyers about what needs to be done as soon as the investigation is underway."

"I'll be thinking about you," she said before she could stop herself.

"I'm always thinking about you, Ashley."

_a_shley fiddled with the bangle on her left wrist and took a breath before pushing through the frosted glass doors of Baine Security. There was nothing to be nervous about. She was just meeting with federal investigators about the illegal actions of her cheating stupid ex. No big deal. It was going to be totally fine.

Then why did she feel so guilty? _She_ wasn't the one attempting to commit a crime.

She smoothed the skirt of her poppy-colored wrap dress and tugged the hem of her navy blazer down. At least she looked put-together.

As instructed, she bypassed the front desk and headed straight up to Jason's office. Mona greeted her warmly and guided her down another hallway. "Don't be nervous," she whispered when they paused outside the conference room. "You'll do just fine."

Ashley gave her a weak smile. She hoped Mona was right. She entered and wondered briefly if vomiting all over the plush carpet would make her testimony less helpful.

Jason stood at the head of the glossy table, deep in conversation with a tall man in a rumpled suit. Eli, who was busy pouring a glass of water for a striking dark-haired woman engrossed in a stack of folders, spotted her first.

"Ms. Sapienza. Thank you for joining us. I understand this is a very difficult time for you."

She felt the warmth of Jason's gaze fall on her, and her cheeks flushed. His expression betrayed nothing, but his eyes burned.

"Ashley." He moved toward her and took her hand in both of his.

It was a small gesture of affection. She wasn't sure if he was sending a message to her or the investigators.

He squeezed her hand before releasing her. "I'd like to introduce you to Lenore Lewis, deputy director of the enforcement division of the SEC." The woman in the charcoal sheath dress glanced over her reading glasses and nodded. "And this is Deion Davis. Mr. Davis is an investigator."

The man extended his hand and shook hers warmly. "Thank you for coming in, Ms. Sapienza. We appreciate your time on this matter."

"It's nice to meet you both," she squeaked. He seemed friendly, but Lenore's scare factor was yet to be determined.

Jason pulled out a chair for her and then took the one next to her. Under the table, his knee pressed against her leg.

"Ms. Sapienza"—Lenore removed her glasses and set them down on the paperwork—"this is just an informal inquiry to see if an investigation is warranted. Are you comfortable talking to us without a lawyer present?"

Ashley glanced at Jason and then nodded. "I think so."

"Very well then, let's start from the beginning." She put her glasses on again. "When did you start to think your fiancé was up to something?"

Ashley took a deep breath and dove in.

She spent the next hour answering questions and clarifying the timeline. Sticking to the facts that Jason had coached her on, she felt reasonably comfortable. Her voice faltered a bit when she explained the catalyst to her ending the relationship. "I don't think I really believed it until I caught him red-handed."

"An understandable reaction," Lenore said simply. "Now I think there's only one last question and we can release you from all this." She gestured with perfectly manicured hands and nodded at Deion.

He cleared his throat and consulted the notebook in front of him. "Ms. Sapienza, if you could just clarify what your relationship to Mr. Baine is."

Ashley felt Jason stiffen imperceptibly beside her. "I'm sorry, you'll have to clarify which Mr. Baine we're discussing. Since there are two in the room."

A chuckle went around the table. Even Lenore cracked a smile.

"I can tell you that if my grandson doesn't have the sense to have his eye on her, I certainly do," Eli said with an exaggerated wink.

"Your grandson has more than enough sense to go with his terrible sense of timing," Jason said mildly. "Ms. Sapienza and I are involved. We were not at the beginning of all this, but we are now. Do you anticipate this posing a problem?"

Lenore studied first Jason and then Ashley for a long moment. "Let's hope not," she said finally. "As long as you can prove that you never met before the party, I don't believe it will be too much of a sticking point.

Ashley sighed quietly. It wasn't the best answer, but it wasn't the worst, either. "So what happens next?" she asked.

Lenore interlaced her fingers. "The information you've brought to our attention warrants a closer look. I can't tell you how long that will take. It could be weeks or even months. However, the cooperation of Mr. Baine and the rest of the company should help speed things along."

"Will I have to testify?"

"It's a definite possibility. Would you be willing to?"

Ashley nodded. "You can compel me to testify even if I wasn't, right?"

"Yes, but it's much easier on everyone when witnesses are willing."

"Is there anything else you need me to do now?"

Deion chimed in. "Not at this point, Ms. Sapienza. Mr. Baine has offered us his services for the investigation, but your part is over for now, unless you come across any new information." He shuffled his papers and closed the folder. "Our investigators work quietly both to ensure that evidence isn't destroyed, or in the case of false information, reputations of individuals and firms remains intact. So the less you say about this, the better."

Ashley didn't give a damn if Steven and Victoria's reputations were smeared like dog crap. "I understand," she said. Jason rose with her.

"If you don't mind, I'll see Ms. Sapienza out." He didn't wait for an agreement but put his hand on the small of her back and guided her out of the room.

Once in the hallway, Ashley allowed herself to sag against the wall. She blew out the breath she felt like she had been holding for an hour. "I'm so glad that's over."

Jason put his hands on her shoulders. "You did an excellent job, Ashley. I can't thank you enough. My family owes you everything. *I* owe you everything."

He pulled her against him, and she breathed him in, running her hands under his jacket. He looked up and down the hallway and pulled her into another door. It was a smaller, more intimate conference room with a round glass table and tall bookcases flanking the lone window.

He leaned against the door to close it, and she heard the quiet snap of the lock. "Don't you have to get back in there?" she asked, eyebrow raised.

"I have a few minutes."

They dove for each other. His mouth crushed into hers as she frantically worked his jacket free. "We can't do this here," she murmured against his mouth.

"Definitely not." His hands streaked up her sides under her blazer. She worked one arm free then the other and dove back into the kiss. They stumbled backwards into the table.

He yanked the tie on her dress open and freed her breast from the cup of her bra. His palm teased her sensitive peak.

She reached for his belt. This was insane. These were not the actions of a normal, sane person, who had just been interviewed by investigators, she warned herself. But how many normal, sane people had the opportunity to enjoy Jason's eager hands and mouth?

She pulled his zipper down and slid her hand inside. He was ready and waiting for her.

"We have to stop." He said it desperately as her fingers closed around his shaft.

She ignored him, working his length with swift strokes. He groaned against her ear, and Ashley found herself being spun around. He forced her down, bending her over the table. The cool glass shocked her bare breast.

He spread her legs with his knee and slid her dress over her hips. Bared to him, she felt his hand gently trail over her exposed curves.

At his mercy, she should have felt submissive, but Ashley only felt powerful.

"What you do to me," he whispered, as he slid his palm

reverently over her cheek, trailing around to her hip. His fingers gripped the cotton edge of her thong, pulling it down her thighs. He left it there, just above her knees and leaned into her, over her.

She pushed against him when she felt his erection nestle at the junction of her thighs.

His arms snaked around her, grasping her breast and freeing the other. And with a deft thrust, he was inside her.

She bit her lip to keep the moan silent. His hands squeezed reflexively as he drove into her again and again. Short, sharp thrusts, each one eliciting a soft grunt from him.

He was lost in her.

She rocked her hips back to meet him. Harder. Faster. Their skin slicked with sweat. Her nipples pebbled against his palms.

He brought a hand between her legs and stroked. The first shudder of his release, deep inside her, brought Ashley to her own.

"My God, Ashley. How do you do this to me?" he whispered against her shoulder, tremors still consuming them.

Straightening, he ran his hands down her sides. "Are you okay? Did I hurt you?"

She sighed against the table, her breath fogging the glass. There were visible face and boob prints. "You're definitely going to have to clean this before your next meeting in here."

He slapped her lightly on the butt before pulling her back to standing. "Have dinner with me tonight."

She turned to face him. "Yes."

He framed her face with his hands. "Where do you want to go? I'll take you anywhere."

"Your house. I'll make dinner."

He dropped a kiss to her mouth. "Perfect. Wait—" He looked concerned. "Can you cook?"

"Very funny." She tied her dress back into place and smoothed the skirt over her legs. "I'll be at your place at seven. Don't be late." She patted his cheek and swept out of the room. "Try not to look like you just had sex when you go back in there," she called over her shoulder.

30

$\mathcal{N}$othing was going to ruin her mood, Ashley decided as she floated across the garage to the elevator. This was a new beginning for her. One worth being excited about.

She heard her name called from a row over and waved to Michael and Mitchell as they approached.

"Well, someone looks smug and happy right now," Mitchell teased.

She felt her cheeks flush. "It's a beautiful spring day. What's not to be happy about?"

"That's not a spring day smile," Michael said, pointing a finger at her face. "There's only one thing that puts a smile like that on someone's face."

She laughed and stabbed the elevator button. "What about you two? You're looking springy yourselves."

Michael held up a shopping tote overflowing with produce. "Farmers market. Mitchell saw a documentary on juicing this weekend."

"It's going to be amazing," Mitchell said, adjusting his glasses.

"Yeah. Kale juice. Amazing." Michael was less enthusiastic. She laughed.

The elevator doors began to slide closed but halted when a man's arm thrust through the opening.

The doors parted, revealing a couple.

Steven. And Victoria.

Ashley stepped back against the wall, the breath vanishing from her lungs. The space seemed to shrink, locking her in with the cheating bastard, the evil arch nemesis. And the knowledge that barely an hour ago she'd told the SEC everything she knew about their illegal activities.

"Oh, goodie," Victoria hummed. She gave Ashley a once over and turned her back on her. Victoria looked stunning as always in a slim-fitting sheath dress the color of her heart: inky black.

"Uh, we can take the next one," Steven said, backing out of the car.

"Great idea," Mitchell said.

"No, we can't." Victoria grabbed Steven's arm and pulled him back in.

Michael and Mitchell moved to flank Ashley while Steven crowded closer to the button panel.

"How about I cook you a nice, romantic dinner tonight, darling?" Victoria purred to Steven, wrapping her arm through his.

Michael cleared his throat dramatically.

"How's your cough, dear? I thought it was getting better." Mitchell winked at his partner.

"Bitch," Michael coughed into his hand. "Horrible person. Ugly shoes."

Victoria spun around, rage etched on her pretty face. She lunged at Michael. Steven caught her inches before her blood red nails raked across Michael's face.

"Pathetic skank," Michael coughed even louder. "Wow, excuse me. It must be bronchitis."

Mitchell patted him on the back. "Come on. How about we get you some nice, romantic cough medicine, darling?"

"What a lovely bag," Ashley said when the doors opened. "I wonder how many ketchup bottles it would take to fill it?"

Steven was too busy trying to contain the irate Victoria to notice when the doors opened and the three of them exited in a fit of laughter.

ASHLEY ARRIVED at Jason's house promptly at seven. She rang the bell and shifted the load in her arms. Jason opened the door before she'd managed to pull her arm back.

"What's all this?" he asked, reaching for the box and bags she carried.

She side-stepped him and hurried through the door. "You answered the door about one second after I rang the bell. Were you hovering?" She set everything down on the foyer table.

He pointed to the chair in the foyer that had a tablet and bottle of water next to it. "I was waiting for you."

"That's very sweet," she said, rising up on her tiptoes to kiss him.

"I've never sat in that chair before. It's not very comfortable," he observed.

She stepped back to look at him. He was still dressed in his suit pants. He had discarded the jacket and tie and rolled up the sleeves of his shirt. She nodded. "Just what I was afraid of. You're inappropriately dressed for our evening plans."

He glanced down at his clothing. "Exactly what are our plans?"

She handed him a gift bag. "These are for you. Consider them your uniform for tonight. Go put them on and meet me downstairs."

"Downstairs? Is this your way of asking for a rematch?"

"You'll see." She gave him a playful shove toward the stairs. "Go change. I'll see you downstairs."

She paused long enough to enjoy the view of him climbing the stairs and then hustled down to the lower level.

When he returned minutes later, he found her plopping steaming slices of pizza on paper plates.

"What do you think? Am I more appropriate now?" He spread his arms.

She grinned. He had changed into plaid pajama pants and a t-shirt. "Very nice." She nodded her approval.

"I see you are following a similar dress code."

She twirled in her sweat pants and long-sleeve college t-shirt.

"This is a test to see if you still have the ability to be human on occasion. Also a reminder that if you expect a girlfriend who lounges around the house in pearls and heels on a Monday night, you'll be very disappointed in me."

"I find that hard to imagine." Jason brought his hands to rest on her hips. "So what are our plans besides pizza and pajamas?"

She handed him the movie she had tucked in the grocery bag. "*Rebecca*," he read.

"It's Alfred Hitchcock and it's amazing," she explained.

"Pizza, pajamas, and a movie. So this is how the other half lives," he quipped, grabbing the plates. "Let's get started then."

They dined on hot, greasy pizza and chips with beer and watched the movie on the huge flat-screen. As the flames consumed Manderley, Jason paused the movie. "What is her name?" he frowned.

"Joan Fontaine?"

"Yes. What's her character's name in the film?"

"Aren't you smart, Mr. Baine?" Ashley wiggled higher into a seated position. "Her character doesn't have a name."

"The main character of the movie is a woman without a name and the movie is named after a woman who isn't even in it?"

She nodded. "It's amazing what just the memory of the presence of a woman can do to a man, isn't it?"

He took a long pull of his beer and pushed play without commenting.

She settled back against him and watched as the flames on the screen licked at the R on the bed.

"Good movie," she sighed.

"Excellent movie."

"How did the rest of your day with the investigators go?" she asked.

"You mean could they tell that I just got done having hot, sweaty sex with a beautiful woman when I went back to the meeting?"

"Pretty much, yeah."

"No one said anything to me, but I didn't realize until after everyone left that my hair was standing up and my fly was down."

Ashley collapsed laughing. "You're joking, right? *The* Jason Baine doesn't walk around with his fly down."

"*The* Jason Baine also doesn't completely lose control during the workday and fuck his girlfriend into oblivion in an empty conference room. I'm not convinced that you're a good influence on me."

"*I'm* not a good influence on *you*? Since I met you, I've spied, I've lied, I've been interviewed by investigators. I've destroyed personal property. And I've been rudely accosted in an office. I think the problem here is you—"

The pillow to her face cut off her argument. "Pretty sure I don't usually start pillow fights either, but in your case, I'll make an exception," he teased.

She recovered from her shock quickly enough to plow a cushion into him, and the war was on.

She went on the attack, and he vaulted over the couch. The battle raged until Ashley ran out of pillows and resorted to using the last weapons she had at her disposal. She flashed him.

He plucked her off of the couch and pulled her down to the floor. "That's not fighting fair."

The kiss was teasing but quickly deepened in intensity. She sighed against his mouth and wrapped her arms around him. *This* was the right way to spend a weeknight.

31

*W*hen she woke in the lonely acreage of Jason's bed, the sun was still low in the sky. He was probably making her breakfast, she thought with a sleepy smile.

She stretched luxuriously and rolled closer to the night-stand to check her phone. She still had fifteen minutes before her alarm, but since she was already awake and scheduled to be at the store by ten, it was a good idea to get moving.

She dressed quickly and padded down the stairs. Jason wasn't in the kitchen, but there was coffee. She helped herself to a mug and wandered in the direction of his office.

The doors to his office were ajar, and she heard voices. She paused, not wanting to interrupt business.

"Off the record, Lenore told me they would be fast-tracking this. I can't afford to have Victoria hovering around the company wreaking havoc for much longer." It was Eli on speakerphone.

"I understand, Grandfather. But it's in the hands of the authorities. I'll do what I can to guide them to the evidence quickly."

"I know," Eli sighed. "But when you get to be my age, you become impatient when it comes to getting what you want, which can be dangerous. I see that trait in you, sometimes."

Ashley peered into the room. Jason had his back to her, his chair swiveled to face the windows behind his desk. He scrubbed a hand through his hair.

"I'm an extremely patient man, Grandfather."

Eli harrumphed. "That's why you decided to cut your weekend short to send that poor girl home early to catch them in the act? That's not patience, my boy. That was a dangerous decision to make. You're very lucky it worked out, but I warn you. Using people like that isn't good for the soul."

Ashley felt icicles form in her belly. Without thinking, she stepped into the room. Jason turned in his chair.

Their eyes met, and she saw the pain she felt mirrored in his face.

"Grandfather, I'll call you back." He hung up the phone and rose.

"You knew." Her voice rang out sharply. "You knew that Steven and Victoria were at the loft."

"Ashley—" He rose.

"You sent me home early on purpose to catch them. Why? Why would you do that, Jason?"

"Ashley, please listen. I couldn't let you go home to him after that weekend."

"So you humiliated me instead?" Every time she stepped foot in this house she was humiliated. Used.

"Ashley—" he tried again circling the desk.

She held up a hand. "Stop. Were you afraid that I was going to tip him off?"

"No. Of course not."

She crossed her arms over her chest.

"How can you be so cold? So manipulative? It's quite calculating to toy with people's lives like this."

"I understand how the situation looks," he began.

"Is this where you deliver the cliché that it's not how it looks and I should believe you instead of my own eyes? That's the cliché, you insufferable ass!"

His jaw clenched, hollowing his cheeks. "I never intended to hurt you."

"Please. What do you care? I'm a pawn. You've been setting me up and manipulating me to get what you want. Well, congratulations. You got everything. You win, Jason."

"My methods were cold. But what I did was necessary for us both," he insisted.

"You used me to get back at Victoria. And not just because of her backdoor dealings with your family's company," she guessed. This wasn't just business. This wasn't even family business. There was an undercurrent here of vengeance sought. "What did she do to you that was so horrible? What did she do that has you so desperate to destroy her?"

Arms folded, his face remained stony.

She stopped her pacing and turned to face him, her shoulders sagging. "It doesn't even matter, does it?" The laugh was bitter in her mouth.

"Everything matters," he said quietly.

"You know what matters to me? I have no home. I may have to testify against my ex-fiancé, who I caught in *my* bed with his mistress. I have been humiliated. And the very worst part is that this is all part of your plan. Do you even care?" Her voice cracked on the word, and she spun around to hide her face.

"Ashley." She heard him cross toward her.

"I'm such an idiot. I didn't even put it together when you

told me your team saw Steven and Victoria leave. They had to be there, watching for something."

Jason held up his hands and took another step forward. "Please, just listen."

"Stay the hell away from me! You made me face them, face what they were doing to me. Just so, what? I wouldn't back down and decide not to testify? Well, guess what. Our 'relationship' is no longer a concern to your stupid investigation, because we no longer have one!"

He took another step toward her.

"Stay away from me! Leave me alone." With that, she turned and fled through the terrace doors.

The smooth stone stairs were cool beneath her bare feet. Ignoring the expansive river view, she hurried in the direction of the driveway. She was going to leave this place behind her forever.

The angry tears fell freely on her cheeks now, and she swiped at them impatiently. She had let herself be humiliated long enough.

Why was it that Jason's betrayal hurt her more than Steven's? Steven was the one who was supposed to love her and be building a life with her. Yet it was Jason's callousness that pierced her heart.

Why was *that* the sucker punch?

The whole thing was a game. From the racquetball court to the cabin. Everything had been planned to gain her trust. What a convincing player Jason was. She shivered despite the sunlight as flashes of him touching her raced through her mind.

It had all felt so real to her. Yet it meant nothing to him.

One thing was sure. She was done with being a pawn. She was also going on an indefinite dating hiatus until she learned to choose men who weren't liars and cheats. Propelled by anger, Ashley stormed away from the house. She had wasted more than enough of her time here.

"Ashley!" Jason's voice called down the path behind her.

The anger spiked. She should run. She should get in her car now and drive away. Maybe take out his mailbox on the way out. But she stood her ground. This was a battle she craved to have.

"Ashley!" He sounded relieved when he spotted her. "Are you okay?"

She let out a short, sharp laugh when he reached for her arm. She yanked away as if he had scalded her. "Don't touch me ever again."

Ignoring her warning, he grabbed for her wrist. "Listen to me. Let me explain—"

"Get this through your thick head, Baine. I don't have to let you do anything. Go find someone else to use." She shoved him, setting him back a half step. She saw the blaze in his eyes. It broke through her anger, awakening something else. Something primal.

Not wanting to dissect it, she whirled away from him and broke into a run toward the river. Stupid, stupid Ashley. She was running away from her car. Away from freedom.

He pounded down the path behind her. Sprinting now, she rounded another bend. There the yard opened to the riverfront and the boathouse.

He was closing in on her, but she kept running.

She should have run faster.

His hand closed on her shoulder yanking her backwards against him. She whirled around in his arms to face him.

"I told you not to run." He wasn't just angry, he was furious.

She gasped for breath, noting his was obnoxiously even.

He shook her once, hard, and she shoved at his chest

without gaining an inch of freedom. He merely tightened his hold on her. They froze that way, with his hands digging into her shoulders and hers fisted against his chest. He was so tall, he all but loomed over her. Now his breathing was as ragged as hers.

"You *will* listen." His grip was bruising.

She put up a respectable fight but found herself flat on her back in the dewy grass with Jason on top of her. He pinned her hands overhead with one hand.

"I am going to kick your ass," she ground out between clenched teeth. It was absolutely absurd. Wrestling a billionaire in his backyard. She might have been nothing but a pawn, a tool, to him, but she was going to make sure he never made that mistake again.

He shifted his hips into hers, and she felt the entire length of his hard-on pressing into her. "Shut up and let me explain."

"You are the worst human being I've ever met," she growled. "And I know Victoria." She hated the fact that her body reacted to his despite the fact that he'd injured her heart.

It was hard to think, or stay livid, with the devil grinding against her.

"I did know that Steven and Victoria were there that morning," he confessed.

"What a nice little joke for you," she snapped.

He clamped his free hand over her mouth. "Shut up." He said it mildly as if asking her to pass the salt. "I couldn't let you go back to him and play house. Not after that weekend. Even if it meant jeopardizing the investigation."

Ashley went still, and he slowly removed his hand.

"How would it have jeopardized anything?" she demanded. "I'd already given you everything off of his computer."

"If you were still with him, you would have become vital to

the case investigators built. They would have asked you to stay, to keep digging, to keep being the dutiful fiancée."

Her stomach turned over at the idea.

"I'm listening," she said as haughtily as her current position allowed.

"I couldn't stand the thought of saying good-bye to you and sending you home to him. The thought of you sleeping next to him..."

He cleared his throat. "I couldn't let that happen. So I did what I do best and manipulated the situation to get what I wanted."

"Why didn't you just ask me not to go back?"

"Because if you left suddenly, they, or Victoria at least, would have been suspicious. She might have tried to delay their plans."

"So you wanted to tie them up in a bow for investigators and keep me all to yourself?" she summarized.

"Yes."

"And you expect me to believe that you care about me?" She was getting angry again. Very, very angry.

"This," he pressed against her, "is real. What you make me feel is real. What I make you feel is real."

"What you make me feel is hurt and betrayed and angry. Also stupid."

"You're not stupid. And that's not all you feel." His hand settled on her belly and need ignited.

"Don't think for a millisecond that just because we had decent sex together that you are entitled to touch me, you elitist asshole."

He groaned and shifted his weight. "Look, I can't concentrate with you writhing under me. If I let you up, will you stay and talk or are you going to take off again?"

"I'll play it by ear." She debated hitting him in the face with an oar from the boathouse.

"Fair enough." He moved off of her and sat next to her.

"You lied to me."

"I didn't lie. I deliberately withheld information."

She rolled her eyes. "If you knew me at all, you'd know that arguing semantics with me is the fastest way to piss me off."

"Ashley." He waited until she turned to look at him. "I'm sorry. Until I met you, there wasn't anything more important to me than destroying Victoria."

"And then along comes a naïve little shopkeeper and suddenly your world changes." Ashley felt like the sarcasm was leaking through her pores.

"Something like that," he said with the ghost of a smile.

"Well, don't stop this fun fiction now. What did Victoria do to make you want to destroy her?"

He gave her a long, sad look. "I don't know if you'll believe me. Especially not now."

"Only one way to find out," she said stubbornly.

32

"*A*shley, no one knows this. I've never told anyone," Jason began.

"I met Victoria when she was 15 and I was 18. It was the summer before I left for college, and my father announced he was getting married. Again. He moved Victoria and her mother into our home right before the wedding.

"She was a beautiful girl already. And she knew it. She used it to get things. And if her looks didn't get her what she wanted, she used other...tools."

He got to his feet and started pacing. Ashley drew her knees to her chest, hating herself for wanting to hear his story. "One night, she came into my bedroom. Started taking her clothes off. She wanted me, she said. But even then, even as a hormone-fueled teenager, I recognized that she was poison. She was 15. She was my stepsister. I made her leave. She tried again and again. The last time I was in the shower, and she came in."

He stopped pacing and stared out over the flowing waters. "She started touching me. I was 18 in a shower with a naked girl wrapping herself around me..."

Ashley's stomach clenched.

"I almost let it happen. But she looked at me and had this look of triumph in her eyes, and I knew I was about to give her a weapon."

"So you stopped her."

Jason nodded. "I stopped her. I pushed her out into the hallway, wet and naked. I told her she was nothing to me but a little girl with daddy issues and I shut and locked the door in her face."

She assumed that Teenage Victoria hadn't taken the rejection well.

"She pounded on the door, screaming. Saying I'd be sorry. She'd make me pay. By the time our parents came home she seemed normal again, and I thought it was settled. Over. But it wasn't. She started…"

He paused and took another deep breath. He came back and sat down next to Ashley, careful not to touch her. He ran his hands over his thighs. Up and down.

"She started doing things," he said finally. If he was acting, she had to hand it to him. He was very, very good.

"What kind of things?" she asked.

"Once, I found pictures in my nightstand. They were of her naked, tied to my bed. She looked scared. I don't know how she took them." He shook his head and ran a hand through his hair. "I confronted her about them. And she got that look again in her eyes. She told me that if I didn't do everything she asked, she would tell our parents that…that I was raping her."

Ashley closed her eyes and fought the sickness growing in her belly.

"I started locking my room every time I left. I found her favorite t-shirt in the backseat of my car ripped open like someone had shredded it."

"Did you tell your father?"

Jason shook his head. "Why would he believe me? It would have been her word against mine, and I didn't think he would take my side over his new wife's. She started making me do things for her. Covering for her when she lied. I took the blame when she wrecked my father's car. I even paid her fine when she was busted for underage drinking. I was living a nightmare in my own home."

Ashley tried to quash the teeny, tiny, infinitesimal spark of sympathy.

"When I left for college, I thought it would finally stop. By that time, she had other targets in her sights. I thought she would forget and finally leave me alone. To be safe, I stayed away. I went to college out of state and took summer jobs there so I wouldn't have to come home," he explained.

Chased out of his own family by a diabolical sociopath. That stupid spark was getting bigger, burning brighter.

"During my junior year, I met someone," he continued. "Her name was Jordan. It got serious. We started talking about our lives after college. And for the first time since my father married Victoria's mother, I started to feel hopeful about the future. And then I made a mistake. I brought her home on Christmas break to meet the family."

He plucked a blade of grass from the ground and rolled it between his fingers.

"Victoria pretended to befriend Jordan. I was terrified to leave them alone together. But Victoria arranged a girls' day out, and I couldn't say no without looking like a control freak to everyone. When they came back, Jordan was in tears. She packed her things and told me she never wanted to see me again.

"Victoria drove her to the airport, and when she returned, she told me what she did. She told Jordan that I had been sexually abusing her for years and that she felt strong enough to tell Jordan the truth because she wanted to save her from the same fate."

That rat bastard Victoria deserved worse than a purse full of ketchup. She deserved prison, an itchy, unflattering jumpsuit for the best years of her life, Ashley thought.

"Jordan transferred to a different school, and I never saw her again. My father and Victoria's mother divorced shortly thereafter. But it wasn't because he was sleeping with just any coked-up socialite. It was because he slept with Victoria."

She gasped, unable to remain silent anymore. "He did *what*?"

"She got him drunk one night when her mother was away on one of her spa trips. It was right before Victoria turned 18. She did it to get back at her mother for something stupid. She'd said no to a summer in Europe or a new car. It was all a game to her. Self-destruct her mother's marriage, treat people like puppets. In the end, my grandfather made a payout to her and her mother to keep them quiet. But she just kept coming back. That's why she works at his company."

He picked up a small stone and tossed it into the river with restrained violence.

"She's dangerous, and she won't hesitate to bite the hand that feeds her."

He dropped his gaze to the ground, kicked at the grass.

"She thought she won the day she talked to Jordan, but she didn't realize what an enemy she had made. I've been waiting for this opportunity since I met her. I am so close to finally being free. But I need you. I need your help to make this happen."

"Why did Jordan believe Victoria over you?" Ashley crossed her arms.

"Victoria is very convincing. She can turn on the tears

214

better than any actor. It took years before my grandfather started to see through her."

"How do I know any of this is true?" She already knew it. But she'd been wrong so many times before.

He grabbed her hand and squeezed. She didn't pull away but kept it as an option. "Ashley, you know it is. You know it the same way you know how I feel about you."

"How do you feel about me, Jason? That I'm useful? That I'm a naïve idiot?"

"I want you and need you. I can't stop thinking about you. Do you know how many times I've lost my train of thought in meetings because I was wondering what you were doing? If you were thinking about me?"

"Don't you mean you lost your train of thought thinking about how useful I've been to you? How I helped you get exactly what you want?" She wasn't fishing for compliments. She wanted the truth. The hard, painful, jagged truth that couldn't be sugarcoated.

He leveled his gaze at her. "I love you, Ashley. And I'm not going to let you go. I will fight for you. I will do whatever it takes to prove to you that you have my heart and that you can trust me."

"*Now* you *love* me?" She gritted her teeth. "You choose to tell me you love me at this exact second, and I'm supposed to believe that you're not being manipulative as hell?"

He held her hand to his heart. "I don't care how it seems. It's the truth. I want to have a life with you, but I can't have that life with Victoria around. She will hurt you to hurt me. She'll use you like she uses everyone. And I can't let that happen."

"You can't control everything, Jason. You can't just force things to work out the way you want them to."

"I just need—"

"Oh, no. It's my turn now. I appreciate how hard it is for you to open up about this. But I want you to understand that just like it's hard for you to trust, you've made it impossible for me to trust you. I'm not a pawn. And neither are you."

Ashley stood up.

"Please don't leave," he whispered.

"Jason, you can't be consumed by revenge for years and then expect to just build a new life once it's finally over. What do you think is going to happen? You're just going to cross Get Back at Victoria off your to-do list and then suddenly you'll become human again?"

He looked vulnerable, nearly human now. She shook her head and looked away. Even after everything, it hurt her to see him in pain.

"I'll give you anything. Don't leave."

"You know what I want?"

He stood and gripped her arms. "Whatever it is, it's yours."

"Time," she said. "And space."

"That's...fair." His gaze bore into her like he was trying to read the inner workings of her soul. "How much?"

She stepped back, out of his grasp. "No contact."

"Ashley."

She held up a hand. "No contact," she repeated.

"Until when?"

"Until I decide."

He shook his head. "I'll give you thirty days."

"You're dictating to me the time I need to heal?"

"I've just gotten a glimpse of what kind of life is possible for us, and you expect me to just let it go without a fight? I'm not willing to do that. I will give you some time and space as you asked. But not forever. I love you."

33

Three weeks later

The flower garden smell hit Ashley the second she opened the door.

"There you are! These came for you today," Mrs. Menifield chirped from the kitchen. The crystal vase on the counter held the most vibrant shade of blood red roses Ashley had ever seen.

"This one said 'Twenty-one.'" Mrs. Menifield handed over the already-opened card. "And there are twenty-one of them!"

Ashley allowed herself a moment to bury her face in the blooms. One moment of fantasy. She had thought the thirty days was a joke. Or at the very least thought Jason would forget and move on and she'd be too busy putting her life back together to notice or looking for nunneries to join.

It hadn't happened that way.

She hadn't forgotten. In fact, she found herself lost in consuming fantasies about Jason more often than was comfortable. And given the floral jungle in Mrs. Menifield's apartment, he hadn't forgotten either.

She hadn't had any contact with him, but the flowers started that first morning. And now Mrs. Menifield's apartment looked like a very expensive wedding venue.

"I'm sorry about turning your home into a flower shop," she sighed.

The woman patted Ashley's arm. "You and your flowers are welcome here as long as you need."

"Thank you, Mrs. Menifield."

She took the blooms into her bedroom and put them on the nightstand. As hurt as she was, she still wanted to feel close to him. He had kept his word. There had been no texts, no phone calls, no visits to the store. Sometimes, she wondered if he logged into the cameras in the shop to watch her.

The truth was, she missed him. When Deion called to let her know that they would be taking Steven into custody, she wanted to reach out to Jason but didn't. Instead, she waited in the parking garage alone so she could watch a team of law enforcement march Steven out in cuffs.

The idiot had the gall to look relieved to see her. "Ash! There's been a mistake! I need you to call Victoria for me. Tell her there's a mistake. Call my lawyer!"

She had shaken her head sadly as he was led to a dark SUV. Call Victoria? The man wanted his ex-fiancé to work with his shitty mistress to get him out of the consequences of his decisions.

"The only mistake here is how much time I wasted on you," she called after him.

She wanted to tell Jason about how the color left Steven's face when Deion oh so coolly said, "Thanks for your cooperation, Ms. Sapienza."

But she didn't. She stayed radio silent and tried to bury herself in work.

Unfortunately, Jason was never far from her thoughts. She didn't doubt his story about Victoria and her heart broke for the 18-year-old forced to sign a deal with the devil. Because of Victoria, he had been cut off from his family and lived his life in constant fear.

But that didn't mean that she could trust him. He'd used her in a vendetta, and she couldn't just sweep that under the rug no matter how many lovely bouquets he sent. How was she supposed to move forward from that?

How could she be with a man whose entire life was consumed by another woman? The thirty days were almost up, and she was no closer to an answer.

Her phone rang, and she dove for it. Every ring, every text she jumped to see if it was Jason. But it never was.

"Hey, Deion, good news on the investigation?" Ashley said.

"Not really. We're a little stalled here. Victoria has covered her ass pretty carefully, so even with Steven turning on her, it's not enough to bring her in."

"So she gets to keep wreaking havoc until when?"

"That's what I wanted to talk to you about. I had an idea. How would you feel about playing a direct role in busting Victoria?"

She flopped back on her bed. "Go on."

He briefly outlined the plan.

"Is this Jason's idea?"

"No, actually I broached it to him, and he said an emphatic no. I tried to tell him that with this small of a window, this is our best bet in bringing it to a close fast, but he said something about using you as bait is never going to happen and then very politely threw me out of his office. By the way, he doesn't look good."

She sat up. "Really?" Somehow the thought of Jason suffering as much as she was cheered her up.

"My question for you is, do you think it will work and are you willing?"

"Do you have time for coffee?"

34

"I am so freaking excited about this," Cara said, calmly sipping an extra dirty martini.

She was statuesque in a fuchsia halter dress and matching heels.

"Please tell me that you wake up in the mornings looking like garbage," Ashley teased.

"Honey, it took me almost 45 minutes just to wiggle into this dress. And don't even ask how long it took to get my hair just right." She gave Ashley the once-over. "You're looking pretty amazing yourself, right now."

Ashley smoothed a hand down her body-hugging strapless dress the color of the roses Jason sent. "Gotta look the part, right? Let's get this show on the road and take down a hell bitch."

They clinked glasses and headed toward the bar.

Ashley nodded imperceptibly in the direction of a broad-shouldered man nursing a scotch. He was checking his very expensive gold watch. "That's him," she whispered.

Cara nodded. They sidled up to the bar next to the man and ordered another round of drinks.

"So speaking of crazy friends," Cara said, loud enough for the man to overhear. "How is your batshit crazy girl, Victoria?"

Ashley rolled her eyes and sighed dramatically. "Van Camp? Oh, don't even get me started on her. She is seriously one bad choice away from being involuntarily committed."

"Dish, girl. You know I love her drama."

Ashley felt the man next to her perk up at the mention of Victoria's name.

"Well," she leaned in but didn't lower her voice. "You know how she's set up in her grandfather's firm, doesn't actually work there, has a bogus title, yadda yadda..."

"Um hmm." Cara nodded. "Tell me how to get *that* job!"

"All you have to do is sleep with the CEO at your old job and then threaten to tell his wife and board of directors everything. She almost got arrested for extortion—oh, and a little embezzlement—until Grandpa stepped in and smoothed things over. He paid them off and then set her up in this fake role just to keep an eye on her. Anyway, she decides that she doesn't make a big enough paycheck for not doing anything and decides to scam this finance guy, Rocco, Rick, Rico...something like that."

"How?"

"Oh, she's pulling some fake insider trading bullshit to leverage this guy into giving her a job at his company."

"Diabolical! Is she banging him, too, to keep him invested?" Cara snorted.

Ashley nodded. "Probably. That's her MO. The stories she tells us at Pilates are ridiculous! She is the friend that no one would be surprised to see get arrested."

"Excuse me for interrupting," the man on Ashley's right said, "but your friend sounds like a whack job."

"You're not kidding," Ashley agreed. "Have you ever known a woman like that? You know, someone who will do anything to get what she wants, even if it means destroying someone."

"I've known one or two." He took a sip of scotch. "So what does she get out of this deal? Or does she just get off on messing with people?"

Cara laughed. "Oh, she definitely gets off on messing with people. She told us once that in order to control people she purposely shows up late to meetings and tells them it's because insert-name-of-corporate-big-wig wanted to meet with her to get her opinion on whatever, and the meeting ran late."

"Well, get this—" Ashley reached for her fresh drink. "Not only was she playing this Rocco/Rick guy, she was also running a similar play on one of her co-workers, I think his name was Steven. He pissed her off a few months ago, so she decided to mess with him. Promised him a fancy job at the new company and this and that. Well, the guy wasn't very careful and just got picked up by the SEC this week!"

Cara whistled, eyebrows sky-high.

"That's pretty serious," the man said.

"She said she's not worried. Said once she closes this deal, she'll be in the clear and can just throw Rocco under the bus for anything. Or extort him with another fake pregnancy scheme."

"You know I always figured she'd get arrested for murder or burning down an ex-husband's house. Insider trading sounds kind of tame for her," Cara said.

Ashley laughed. "Give her time. She never disappoints, especially when she's off her meds."

"Ladies, it was a pleasure." The man stood and straightened his jacket. "The next round is on me." He peeled off two twenties from his billfold and threw them on the bar before hurrying off.

Cara and Ashley dissolved into giggles.

"Oh, that was fun," Ashley gasped. "Can we do this every weekend?

"Did you see his face when you mentioned his name?" Cara hooted.

Ashley's phone signaled a text.

"Okay, here comes round two. Let's catch up soon!" She took another sip for courage and slid off the barstool.

"Good luck," Cara called after her.

ASHLEY SPOTTED her quarry right where she was supposed to be, on the sidewalk outside the bar. She paused to take a deep breath. "Here goes nothing," she whispered.

Victoria Van Camp was pacing the hallway on her cell phone.

"Dammit, Steven. Answer the fucking phone!" She hung up and started to redial.

"Oh, honey, I don't think he's taking your calls anymore," Ashley said, brushing past her.

Victoria looked up. Her eyes narrowed to slits. "Oh really, and why is that?"

Ashley shrugged daintily. "Haven't you heard? We got back together. Well, he *thinks* we're back together." She winked. "He thought that staying with me and cooperating with the SEC was a better idea than being your little toy."

"You're lying." Victoria spat out the words and stepped closer.

"Am I? Let me guess, you haven't heard from him since Tuesday. Right?"

She saw it. The flash of worry in the viper's eyes for just a split second.

"My, my. That seems like a long time for someone to ignore you, Victoria. Speaking of ignoring you, is Rocco Embry returning your calls?"

The color drained from Victoria's face. "What are you talking about?" Clutching her phone, she started to dial.

Ashley smiled. "Oh, you'll find out soon enough. If you'll excuse me, I'm going to pop by my store. You know, some of us actually have jobs. Give my best to Rocco."

She sailed past Victoria without a backward glance.

"Are you still here, Rocco? I'm running late. Eli Baine wanted to meet with me about—Hello? Hello?"

35

She was waiting for her car at the valet stand when her phone rang. "Great job, kid," Deion said in her ear. "We picked up Rocco on his way out of the bar as he was hanging up on Victoria. She's blowing up his phone as we speak."

Ashley did a little shimmy. "Man, that feels good!"

"That was a nice touch with the whole 'running late name drop' scenario."

"I figured that as long as Eli did what he said he would to delay her, it would be another nail in the coffin."

"Nicely done. You need anything else, you know what to do."

"Thanks, Deion. See you around."

She tipped the valet and slid behind the wheel of her car. She felt good. Now there was only one thing left to do. Well, maybe two.

She parked on the side street by the alley behind the store and used the back door, remembering to re-arm the alarm once she was inside.

How many times in the past few weeks had she looked at the cameras and wondered if Jason was watching her?

She wondered how he would react when he heard about Victoria and Rocco. He probably wouldn't be very happy with Deion and the rest of the team once he found out they had gone behind his back. But the fact that he'd refused to use her as bait had given her the answer she needed.

In the office, she switched on the desk lamp and the electric kettle. A nice cup of tea might help soothe her nerves.

She heard the clink of metal at the back door, and her pulse jumped. Someone was trying to pry the door open. Ashley grabbed her bag and hurried down the hallway, away from the door and onto the store floor. She dug for her phone, started to dial 911.

"Put it down."

Victoria strolled in, twirling a small crowbar.

Blindly, Ashley pushed what she hoped was the last button on her phone.

"What are you doing here? How did you get in?" She demanded.

"I thought it was time we had a little chat," Victoria drawled.

Shit. Shit. Shit. They'd all underestimated Victoria.

"I don't have anything more to say to you." Ashley crossed her arms and pretended she wasn't gravely concerned that a crowbar-wielding maniac wanted to talk.

"Oh, I think we have a lot to talk about," Victoria said menacingly. "Do you realize what kind of enemy you've made?"

"Seeing what a mess you've made of your little inside trading deal, I'm not really concerned with your follow-through."

"The mess *I* made? Everything was fine until you stuck your ugly little nose into my business. Rocco will make this deal, and I will make you pay for your pathetic attempt to slow me down."

"What about Steven?"

"Keep him." Victoria shrugged. "I got what I needed from him, and now you can have what's left."

"This deal wouldn't have been possible without Steven. You're just going to cut him out of it now?"

"Is that what he told you? That he did all the work?" she sneered.

"If he hadn't told you about Phil—"

"You think it had to be Phil Barden? Or Steven? Or Rocco? Don't be stupid. I could have made this deal with anyone for any information. Steven and Phil and the Tundra merger were all just handy."

"You just use people, don't you? You find a weapon and you exploit it."

Victoria took another step forward. Ashley held her ground.

"I do what I have to to get what I want."

"What about Jason?"

"What about my dear stepbrother?"

"You lied about him. You threatened him. You blackmailed him."

Victoria threw her head back and laughed. "Men are so simple. Either you reward them with sex or you threaten them with it. So he told you about us then. You two have gotten awfully close, haven't you?"

"There is no 'us' between you and him."

"He's lived the last ten years in total fear of what I am willing to do to destroy him. Every decision he makes is because of me. You tell me if that's not an 'us.'"

"You tortured him in his own home," Ashley accused.

Victoria shrugged. "He said no to me. So I decided to make him regret it."

"You said if he didn't do what you wanted, you would tell your parents that he raped you." Ashley could barely choke out the words.

"Oh, no, dear. I said that if he didn't do what I wanted, I would tell *everyone* that he was raping me. Over and over again. Sexually assaulting his poor little innocent stepsister."

"But he never laid a hand on you."

"I didn't need him to fuck me. I just made it look like he did. Maybe he should have. It would have been much more pleasant for him."

"Why? So he could end up like his father? Paying you off because you got him drunk and banged him when he was practically passed out?"

"I was seventeen years old. Legally a minor."

"Oh, poor little victim Victoria. Your mommy wouldn't let you do something so you decided to bang stepdaddy. That'll teach her."

Victoria laughed. "I wanted to go to Nice for spring break. She said no. And look who went to Nice for the entire summer, had her college education paid for, *and* landed a job at Baine Investments. I always get what I want. Don't get in my way."

Ashley stepped closer. "Or what?"

Victoria swung the crowbar carelessly into the glass counter. It shattered, sending shards in every direction. "Oops."

"You broke in here and now you're destroying private property. That's very classy," Ashley commented.

"Classy is how I'm going to wreck this place and tell everyone it was you. You went crazy because I stole your fiancé. You couldn't handle it."

Victoria swiped her arm across the old farm table, sending hand-thrown pottery flying.

Ashley clenched her hands into fists. "No. Classy is me ruining your deal with Rocco and sending you to jail."

"And just how are you going to do that?"

Ashley pointed to the camera behind the cash register and then the one over the door. "Everything you've said has been recorded, you idiotic piece of dumbass trash."

Victoria paused long enough to take in the cameras, nostrils flaring. And then she launched herself at Ashley, swinging wildly with the crowbar. Ashley blocked it painfully with her left arm and swung with her right.

She felt the satisfying connection with Victoria's perfect blade of a nose. The woman screamed and tackled her to the ground.

Bits of broken glass bit into her back as she fought to get Victoria off her. An elbow glanced off her cheek, and Ashley used the opportunity to shove Victoria in the face. They rolled as one, knocking into a shelving unit, sending more items crashing to the floor.

Victoria ended up on top again, her hands closing around Ashley's neck in a vice-like grip. "I'm going to kill you," she shrieked.

There was blood. Pain. Fear. But mostly fury. Directed at this woman who so carelessly destroyed whatever others valued. The fury fueled Ashley, and she fought.

Then there were lights and voices. And hands.

Thank God, Ashley thought, as Victoria's hands were pried off her throat.

Strong arms lifted her from the ground. "You okay, Ashley? That was some show." Deion steadied her.

"Please tell me you heard every word," Ashley rasped, bending at the waist to catch her breath.

"Every single word. She's done. She's going away for a long time."

She glanced around. "I didn't think she was going to do this much damage. Barbara is going to be so pissed."

"She broke my fucking nose!" Victoria, restrained by two officers, shrieked. Blood trickled from her face onto her chest, giving her a demonic look.

"I've been wanting to do that since I met her," Ashley admitted.

"She attacked me! I was defending myself!" Victoria howled.

Ashley turned her back on the scene and grabbed a box of tissues off the counter. She had what felt like a million little cuts everywhere. Her cheek ached, and her neck burned from Victoria's hands.

"Ashley!"

Her heart skipped a beat at the voice.

Jason pushed his way through the crowd, rushing her. His fingers roamed her face, her arms, her torso. "Are you okay? Are you hurt?"

She saw it, the panic, the fear in his eyes, and felt tears prick her own.

"Jason." She framed his face in her hands. "I'm fine. I'm okay."

"You're bleeding."

"It's mostly Victoria's."

"You're bleeding," he said again. "Your face."

"Jason, I'm fine. Everything is fine. It's all over."

Deion came up and slapped Jason on the back. "Congratulations, Mr. Baine. Your batshit crazy stepsister is going to jail."

Jason rounded on him. "I said you were not to use Ashley as bait."

Deion held up his hands, and Ashley stepped between

them. "Jason, stop. Listen." She pushed him back a step. "I'm fine, and Victoria is going to jail."

His gaze flew back and forth between Deion and Ashley. Deciding, he pulled her into him. "You scared me. I saw her break in on the monitors, and I couldn't get here fast enough."

"I knew you were watching."

"You didn't say I couldn't check up on you. That doesn't count as contact."

She laughed and buried her face in his chest. "No, no, it doesn't."

"Are you sure you're okay?"

"I'm better than okay. I love you, Jason Baine."

He clutched her to him. "Say it again."

"I love you."

"Again."

"I love you, Jason, and you're finally free." She pulled back and looked into his eyes. "She confessed to everything. We recorded every word."

"Everything?"

She saw the understanding begin to dawn in his eyes.

"Everything. She'll never be able to hold those lies over your head again."

He crushed her to him again. "You love me and you freed me," he murmured against the top of her head. "I'm never letting go of you again."

"So you're not mad?"

"Oh, I'm furious. You deliberately put yourself in danger."

"To be fair, I didn't really think she was going to bring a crowbar in here."

"Never underestimate crazy."

"I'm crazy about you," she said.

"Say it one more time," he insisted, holding her just a little tighter.

"I love you, Jason." Her voice was muffled against his chest.

"I love you, Ashley Sapienza. I think we should get married."

"Right now?" she teased. "Don't you think we could find a better venue?" She glanced around at the police, the flashing lights, the sparkle of broken glass.

Jason started to sink before her. She gripped his arms. "Don't you dare! I forbid you to propose!"

He paused, mid-knee. "You're going to say it, aren't you?"

"I need time."

"You're killing me, Ashley. First you use yourself as bait. Then I watch you get attacked. Then you tell me you need more time."

"I literally just took one engagement ring off. You can't expect me to just slap on another one and hope for the best!"

"That's exactly what I expect. I even have the ring."

"Shut up. You do not," she argued.

He tapped his jacket pocket. "Next to my heart."

"Stop it. Do *not* get all swoony and romantic on me! We barely know each other. We're all adrenalized and enamored. We need to take our time and think things through."

"I'm tired of thinking. I'm tired of having my life on hold. I'm tired—" His entreaty was interrupted by Victoria.

"I'm going to kill every single one of you," she howled as she was hauled through the front door by two officers.

"Maybe this isn't the best moment," Jason agreed, watching her go.

"Yeah. You think?" Ashley joked. "Besides, you seem more like a champagne and flowers kind of guy. Not the broken glass and raving lunatic type."

"You may have a point," he admitted.

"It's not a no, by the way," she told him.

"How much time do you need?" He reached into his jacket and produced the box. Her eyes were drawn to it magnetically.

"Um. I don't know. This is a big deal. I should live on my own first. Then we should live together. Figure out if you can stand me leaving empty yogurt containers everywhere and if I can handle you talking about balance sheets in your sleep. We should talk about kids and dogs and retirement funds."

He opened the box, and Ashley blinked. It was a vintage solitaire wrapped in a halo of smaller, yet no less spectacular, diamonds.

"Gah."

"So thirty days then?" he suggested smugly.

She nodded for nearly a minute. "Yeah. Thirty days should do it."

"I know it's crazy," he said softly. "But just because it's crazy doesn't mean it isn't exactly right. Because this is."

She continued nodding until he snapped the box shut. "This is insane," she said, still staring at the box. "Right?"

There was the sound of breaking glass from outside and more screaming.

"But not *that* insane," Jason said.

Ashley grinned. "Are you ready for the next chapter?"

He stroked a hand over her cheek. "In thirty days." And when he kissed her, it all felt exactly right.

Jason gave Ashley her thirty days.

He helped her move out of Mrs. Menifield's place and into a nice one-bedroom with a view of the river three blocks from Dwell.

He slid the ring on her finger at 12:01 a.m. on the thirty-first day... after Ashley said yes, of course.

It turns out he'd purchased the apartment in Ashley's name. She is now a landlord with a very nice side income.

In their spare time, they took up competitive racquetball in a local league.

Ashley's parents always hated Steven. They welcomed Jason with open arms.

Jason became a comfy clothes aficionado.

Ashley hasn't had to put ketchup in anyone's designer purse since.

They got two dogs and decided two or three kids would be nice someday...

Steven was found guilty and served six months in a white-collar prison where he lost his tan but gained a few "new" skills. He was arrested and imprisoned again a year after he was released for committing insurance fraud involving timeshares in Florida.

Victoria also served time in prison. After thirteen months, she was released and then arrested in the same day. Snitched out by her cellmate, she was caught driving toward the lake house with a trunk-load of arson supplies, a shovel, and an internet search history that included such gems as "where to bury bodies." She is in jail, awaiting trial for lots and lots of charges. Three attorneys have quit or been fired. She is now representing herself.

EPILOGUE

*A*shley spun her chair away from her desk to stare out the window. The summer night was just beginning with a spectacular sunset. She could hear the cacophony of crickets through the open balcony door. On a contented sigh, she wiggled her bare toes into the plush carpet beneath her feet.

As a wedding present, Jason had turned one of the upstairs guest rooms into a spacious home office.

She admired the sparkle of her rings under the light from the desk lamp. She was Mrs. Baine. He slid the wedding ring on her finger in front of a small crowd of friends and family in an intimate ceremony at the lake house.

And now? Now, she lived in a home with a racquetball court and woke up every morning next to Jason. They dined outside picnic-style most nights after long days at work and launched kayaks from the backyard on the weekends. Next week she would be joining him on a business trip to Rome. It would be her second European trip since the wedding.

She had watched Jason loosen up millimeter by millimeter into a new life, one free from Victoria and her threats.

Theirs was a good life.

"What's going through your mind, Mrs. Baine?"

She swiveled to face him. Jason leaned against the doorway. With his sleeves rolled up and feet bare, he was the picture of relaxed.

She rose to greet him with a kiss. "You caught me. I was just thinking about how lucky I am."

"Good, because there's something I want to talk to you about." He produced a stack of papers from behind his back and handed them to her.

She crinkled her nose at the legal documents. "It's kind of late for a prenup since we're already married."

He gave her a look of mock exasperation. "It's not a prenup. Read, please." He tapped the pages with a long finger.

She skimmed the first page. "What is this?"

"It's a purchase agreement for Dwell."

"You're buying the store?"

"No. You are."

"What do you mean I'm buying it? The store is mine? What about Barbara?"

"Barbara was interested in retiring, and I was interested in your future."

"You two discussed this without even consulting me?"

"I wanted to surprise you. Consider it a belated wedding present."

"And what is that brand new SUV in the garage then?"

"An engagement present."

She bit her lip to keep from smiling. "You're doing it again. You're swooping in and interfering with my life. Have you learned nothing?"

"I think you mean *our* life. And there was no swooping. I am incapable of swooping. I am very dignified in my movements. Barbara approached me, and you of all people know the store is a sound investment. Would you rather work for some stranger who buys Barbara out or do you want to work for yourself?"

"Wouldn't I be working for you?"

"This is your store. This is your name on the agreement."

"That's a lot of zeros to have my name attached to."

"You forget what resources you have available to you. What's mine is yours." He tucked a stray strand of hair behind her ear and put the papers on her desk. "I want you to be happy, Ashley. I want you to have everything."

"Damn, you're good at this."

"Wait, I have one more good point to make before you concede."

"You're pretty cocky, Romeo."

"When we travel, you can use the trips to buy inventory for the store."

He had her and he knew it. It was her dream. She had even scheduled an appointment with a wholesaler in Rome while Jason was in meetings.

"What if I don't want to run Dwell?" she asked with a dainty shrug.

"Then you can do something else and hire someone to run it."

He leaned down and kissed her neck.

"You're trying to distract me."

"Tell me you want it." His lips brushed her jawline. "Tell me it's exactly what you want."

Ashley sighed as he moved to her mouth.

"I want it and I want you. I want it all. It's exactly what I want."

AUTHOR'S NOTE TO THE READER

Dear Reader,

Wow, you guys. This was my very first book! Jason and Ashley and that jerk-wad Victoria are where this whole wild ride started for me. Thank you for picking up Undercover Love and for cheering on Ashley as she went from humiliated fiancée to funny karmic weapon of revenge.

If you loved these two and their scheming, I recommend you check out my standalone romantic comedy The Worst Best Man. Or for more witty romantic suspense (if I do say so myself), grab the sexy Sinner & Saint duet!

Thank you for being awesome! If you enjoyed Undercover Love, I'd love it if you'd consider leaving a review, signing up for my newsletter, or following me on Facebook and Instagram. Or you could send me a platter of tacos. In fact forget everything else. I'll just take the tacos!

Thanks again for reading! Don't stop! (That's what she said. HA!)

Xoxo,
Lucy

ABOUT THE AUTHOR

Lucy Score is a *Wall Street Journal* and #1 Amazon bestselling author. She grew up in a literary family who insisted that the dinner table was for reading and earned a degree in journalism. She writes full-time from the Pennsylvania home she and Mr. Lucy share with their obnoxious cat, Cleo. When not spending hours crafting heartbreaker heroes and kick-ass heroines, Lucy can be found on the couch, in the kitchen, or at the gym. She hopes to someday write from a sailboat, or oceanfront condo, or tropical island with reliable Wi-Fi.

Sign up for her newsletter and stay up on all the latest Lucy book news.
And follow her on:
Website: Lucyscore.com
Facebook at: lucyscorewrites
Instagram at: scorelucy
Twitter at: LucyScore1
Blog at: lucyscore.com/blog
Readers Group at: Lucy Score's Binge Readers Anonymous

ACKNOWLEDGMENTS

Thank you, fantastic human beings, for the following:

- Jessica Snyder for digging into edits on this crazy rewrite.
- Kari March Designs for this delicious new cover design.
- Mr. Lucy for not picking on me too much when it took me almost a full year to re-write and edit this book.
- Taco Bell's Nacho Fries.
- Binge Readers Anonymous for being the best humans ever.
- Sean and Aubrey for taking a chance on a no-name wannabe writer.
- Joyce and Tammy for coming on board #TeamLucy and keeping me on track on a minute-by-minute basis.
- Heather for your excellent taste in quotes and your eagle eye for typos.

LUCY'S TITLES

Standalone Titles

Undercover Love

Pretend You're Mine

Finally Mine

Protecting What's Mine

Mr. Fixer Upper

The Christmas Fix

Heart of Hope

The Worst Best Man

Rock Bottom Girl

The Price of Scandal

The Blue Moon Small Town Romance Series

No More Secrets

Fall into Temptation

The Last Second Chance

Not Part of the Plan

Holding on to Chaos

The Fine Art of Faking It

Where It All Began

Bootleg Springs Series

Whiskey Chaser

Sidecar Crush

Moonshine Kiss

Made in the USA
Middletown, DE
27 July 2022